African-American Folktales for Young Readers

"Well-sourced and well-told, the 30-plus tales in this lively collection are welcome indeed."
— *Publishers Weekly*

"Readers of every ethnicity will enjoy these charming tales of clever children, evil monsters, tricksters, and small animals outwitting powerful foes."
— *Los Angeles Times Book Review*

"An outstanding collection."
— *The Washington Times*

"Certainly, this varied collection has something to offer in its very breadth."
— *School Library Journal*

Storytelling World Honor Winner

An American Bookseller Pick of the List

African-American Folktales for Young Readers

Including Favorite Stories from
African and African-American Storytellers

Collected and edited by
Richard Alan Young
and Judy Dockrey Young

August House Publishers, Inc.
LITTLE ROCK

Printed in the United States of America

10 9 8 7 6 5 4 3 2 1   HC
10 9 8 7 6 5   PB

LIBRARY OF CONGRESS CATALOGING-IN-PUBLICATION DATA

African-American folktales for young readers :
including favorite stories from African and African-American storytellers /
collected by Richard Alan Young and Judy Dockrey Young–1st ed.
          p.   cm.
Summary : A collection of stories from the African-American oral tradition,
presented as they have been told by professional black storytellers from
Rhode Island to Oklahoma.
ISBN 0-87483-308-6 (hb)
ISBN 0-87483-309-4 (pb)
1. Afro-Americans—Folklore. 2. Tales—United States.
[1. Folklore, Afro-American. 2. Storytelling—Collections.]
I. Young, Richard Alan, 1946- . II. Young, Judy Dockrey, 1949-
          PZ8.1.A252   1993
          398.2'08996073—dc20   92-38264

Executive editor: Liz Parkhurst
Project editor: Kathleen Harper
Design director: Ted Parkhurst
Cover design: Harvill Ross Studios Ltd.
Ceramic sculpture: Earnest Davidson
Illustrations: Kenneth Harris

Contents

Introduction

Africanand African-American storytelling has maintained an important position in America since its inception. In the last two centuries a host of performers, poets, historians, folklorists, ethnomusicologists, anthropologists, historians, and just plain folks have lovingly chronicled, created, and nurtured the rich legacy of black stories and storytelling. Their work clearly illustrates the influence Africans and black Americans have had on the New World.

That legacy, however, has not been maintained without a commensurate amount of trials and tribulations. As Professor Daryl Dance reminds us, from the early debacle of American slavery to the present challenges of racism and intolerance, prohibitions against Africans and African Americans continue to make their experience unique:

> Forced into a closed society, often largely lacking in literacy, black Americans developed and maintained an oral tradition probably unmatched, and certainly not surpassed, by that of any other group in America. Their folklore reveals the history of black people in this country and their psychological reactions to their experience. The similarities of themes appearing

throughout their tales, from the slave anecdotes to the contemporary stories, suggest that for black Americans basically very little has changed.[1]

The black oral tradition has been manifested in many ways and was used to serve numerous functions. It was expressed through song—both religious and secular. It was used to interpret the universe; to resolve natural and physical phenomena; to teach morals; to maintain cultural values; to pass on methods of survival; and to praise God. Stories have been used to celebrate freedom as well as to condemn black enslavement. They have chronicled the exploits of criminals, the mischief of the indolent, the wisdom of the elderly, and the courage of heroes. African Americans have protested injustices and gained political hegemony through the use of storytelling. There is no area of the black experience in America that has not been influenced by this vibrant oral tradition. The ability to tell a good story has brought strangers together, validated friendships, and reduced hostilities.

From the time Africans and African Americans were denied the freedom to educate themselves, or even participate in the formulation of their own political, social, and economic well-being, oral communication remained their only opportunity to create a world for themselves—a world fashioned by memory and influenced by the immediate challenges of the moment. Stories communicated their understanding of what was, and their hope of what might be. Lawrence Levine states in his important work, *Black Culture and*

Black Consciousness, the important contribution that oral history and literature have made:

> Upon the hard rock of racial, social, and economic exploitation and injustice black Americans forged and nurtured a culture: they formed and maintained kinship networks, made love, raised and socialized children, built a religion, and created a rich expressive culture in which they articulated their feelings and hopes and dreams.[2]

The tradition has been kept alive by literary artists and scholars like Frederick Douglass, Hariett Jacobs, Paul Lawrence Dunbar, James Weldon Johnson, Langston Hughes, Arna Bontemps, William Wells Brown, as well as contemporary writers and collectors like Julius Lester, Alice Walker, Daryl Dance, Marian Barnes, and Toni Morrison.

A host of anthropologists and folklorists have added to our knowledge. Among them, Zora Neal Hurston reigns supreme. Arguably, this Eatonville, Florida woman did more for the cause of African-American folklore than anyone else at a turbulent time in America's history when many whites looked upon the scholarly contributions of black Americans with jaundiced eye. From her early work entitled *Jonah's Gourd Vine* to *Mules and Men*, Hurston's work has made an indelible imprint on American literature. Understanding its significance is fundamental to recognizing the importance of black folklore. Others such as Sterling A. Brown, John Henrik Clarke, Ellen Terry, and Ann Petry have greatly added to her legacy.

Equally important to the scholarship are a host of African-American storytellers and performers who continue to "tell." This cadre of gifted people is exposing ever-increasing numbers of us to the black oral tradition. Among them are Hugh Morgan Hill, Mary Carter Smith, Jackie Torrence, Linda Goss, Frankie and Doug Quimby, Maya Angelou, Alice McGill, Larry Coleman, and Tejumola Ologboni.

In this fine collection of stories, Richard and Judy Dockrey Young have compiled an assortment of stories, many of which are reminiscent of their own experiences growing up in the southern United States during the 1940s and 50s. While these stories do not reflect the totality of the challenges faced by black Americans during such a turbulent period, they are stories that continue to be told by African Americans because they speak to particular experiences and because the stories themselves have messages that transcend color and culture. They are stories that represent our common experience.

Beyond the attributes mentioned, storytelling has the power to foster understanding and build bridges of respect among cultures. One does not have to look far to realize that our neighborhoods and communities are becoming increasingly diverse. Unfortunately, the many cultures we live among often allow their politics, ideologies, and traditions to create divisions that are divisive, pervasive, and violent. We are truly in need of the kind of healing that storytelling can provide. Its power to break down barriers—and even explain the reasons for those barriers we tend to protect ourselves with—is both unique and wonderful.

The stories in this collection have been gathered with integrity, respect, love, and compassion. They are stories that begin on the continent of Africa and end on the streets of cities and towns throughout America. Henry Louis Gates in his introduction to *Talk that Talk* by Linda Goss and Marian Barnes speaks to the contribution that stories can make:

> The stories that we tell ourselves and our children function to order our world, serving to create both a foundation upon which each of us constructs our sense of reality and filter through which we process each event that confronts us every day. The values that we cherish and wish to preserve, the behavior that we wish to censure, the fears and dread that we can barely confess in ordinary language, the aspirations and goals that we most dearly prize—all of these things are encoded in the stories that each culture invents and preserves for the next generation, stories that, in effect, we live by and through.[3]

As you read these stories, I encourage you to read them out loud. Stand up and experiment with the gestures and movements that each story implies. Vary the meter, the pace, and your vocal inflection. Become the lion, the turtle, Casey Jones, or even Annie Christmas. Explore the full potential of these treasures and let them take you to times and places that have yet to be imagined. Let them inspire, embolden, and motivate you to learn about yourself and the world around you. Let them encourage and evoke in you the desire to carry on the tradition of storytelling by telling your own story. Then use your special gifts to help heal, enlighten, and inform those who are a part of your experience. Stories, after all, are meant to be told. It is in performance that they achieve their greatest power. Through the nuances of the human voice, the expressiveness of the face, the mystery of the eyes, and the manipulation of the body, stories reach their full potential to transform the ordinary into the extraordinary. Find your own voice and allow it to resound until all are convinced, beyond a doubt, that you have "Beautiful Brown Eyes."

—Dr. Rex Ellis
Director, Office of Museum Programs
Smithsonian Institution
Washington, DC

NOTES

1. Daryl Cumber Dance, *Shuckin' and Jivin': Folklore From Contemporary Black Americans* (Bloomington: Indiana University Press, 1978), xvii.

2. Lawrence W. Levine, *Black Culture and Black Consciousness: Afro-American Folk Thought From Slavery to Freedom* (New York: Oxford University Press, 1977), xi.

3. Linda Goss and Marian Barnes, eds., *Talk That Talk* (New York: Simon & Schuster, Inc., 1989), 17.

LANGUAGES REPRESENTED IN THIS BOOK

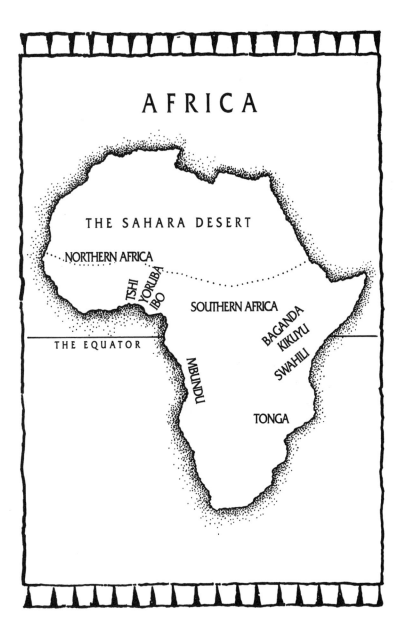

AFRICA

THE SAHARA DESERT

NORTHERN AFRICA

TSHI
YORUBA
IBO

SOUTHERN AFRICA

BAGANDA
KIKUYU

SWAHILI

THE EQUATOR

MBUNDU

TONGA

Languages of Africa

The African continent is huge: it is over a million square miles larger than North America. (Africa is about 11,700,000 square miles in area.) Ancient people of Europe knew about the people and cultures of northern Africa from Egypt westward to Morocco. Northern Africa and Europe had trade and political relations from the beginning of recorded history. But the people of Europe were largely ignorant of just how big Africa was, and of how many different kinds of people lived there, until the 1700s. The enormous Sahara, the largest desert in the world, separated northern Africa from southern, or sub-Saharan Africa. The desert prevented Europeans from visiting sub-Saharan Africa until the last three centuries.

Sub-Saharan Africa is a vast range of every kind of land, from desert to swamp, from snow-covered mountains to lush rain forests. In the southern half of the African continent, over eight hundred languages are spoken. Each language group has its own history and culture, its own ceremonies and dances and songs and stories. When the European travelers first encountered this rich diversity, they sometimes called the languages they encountered by the wrong names.

Oftentimes they mispronounced or misspelled the names of language groups, and other times they used a name from one language to identify the language of an enemy group.

As a result, some language groups in southern Africa are commonly known by names that are inaccurate but widely used today. Because they are well-known, we have used the commonly accepted names for language groups represented in this book.

While each different language group of people was once isolated by distance and geography from other groups, many languages such as Swahili have spread across vast areas of the continent. Swahili, or Ki-Swahili, means "coastal people." That language has spread from one small area to most of the southeastern portion of Africa. Swahili and Kikuyu, which are represented in this book, are subdivisions of a larger family of languages once known as Bantu. Some linguists, or language scientists, now call this language group Benue-Congo.

The people who speak the Bantu languages—there are over a hundred such languages—have migrated far over the centuries and carried their languages with them across the eastern, central, and southern parts of sub-Saharan Africa. Just as people and languages moved about, so did the stories, and often one story may be told by a dozen different language groups.

Most of the sub-Saharan African people who came to America were from the western equatorial coast of Africa, and represented a fairly limited number of language groups, especially Tshi, Yoruba, Ibo, Mbundu, and Tonga.

Young Heroes
and Heroines

Young readers thrill at stories of brave young people like themselves who face difficult dangers with great courage and strength. These stories become the most popular ones with young listeners, and are asked for most often in storytelling sessions.

Just as all these stories originated in Africa, and were then brought to America later, so this section of our collection begins with two stories that are told more often in Africa, followed by four stories that were brought to America later and are told primarily in the South.

Since young listeners often ask for scary stories, as well as stories about young heroes and heroines, it is not surprising that most of these folktales tell of a ghost or monster who threatens the ready, willing, and able young characters at the center of these adventures.

Beautiful Brown Eyes

Retold from folklore and inspired by the stories of Len Cabral, this story originally came from the Yoruba-speaking people of West Africa.

In Bénin, along the Ouémé River on the Atlantic coast of equatorial Africa, lived a lovely maiden with beautiful brown eyes. She had the most beautiful brown eyes in her village, perhaps the most beautiful brown eyes in all the world. Every young man who happened to see her eyes when she walked through the village was captured by their beauty. Old men with wives admired her eyes and talked of what beautiful children she would have, and how fortunate would be the young man whom she would someday marry.

In the season when the girl with the beautiful brown eyes came of marrying age, a great and terrible drought came upon the land. No rain had fallen for months, and when the rainy season came, it was not rainy at all. Only hot wind blew, and the sun beat down on the village without mercy. First the leaves began to wilt, then the ground began to dry and crack. Then the crops and forest began to die, and the river Ouémé began to go dry. Soon the river was only brown mud and the mud was far down the slippery bank. There was no clean water to drink, and the people began to be thirsty.

When the girl should have been making plans for a wedding, she was instead climbing up and down the banks of the river, filling a jar with muddy water that she dipped carefully in a gourd from the muddy pools where the river had been. Each day she made many trips to the drying riverbed, and the water she carried back saved the lives of many of her family and friends in the village. Other girls were also going for water, but she seemed to find more because she was very dutiful and did as her parents had asked her to. She worked slowly and lovingly, letting the gourd rest in the mud and fill very slowly with the precious water.

At last, however, even she could find no water to drink.

One morning, as she stood in the mud of the riverbed, she began to cry, because she could find no water clear enough to take into the jar. One of her tears hit the mud, and up out of the mud came a beautiful fish. He had beautiful brown eyes.

"Give me your jar, and I will fill it for you," said the fish.

At first she was afraid, but the fish spoke so kindly, and had such beautiful, sad eyes, that at last she lowered her jar toward him, wondering how he would take it from her without any hands.

The fish did not take the jar, but put his mouth over the mouth of the jar and spewed cool, clear water into the jar until it was full! Then the fish sank back into the mud without a word.

When she returned to the village, everyone wanted to know where she had found such clear water, but she did not tell them, for she was afraid they would accuse her of lying if she told them the truth.

The following day she returned to the same place, and again the fish appeared out of the mud.

"Give me your jar, and I will fill it for you," he said again, and she held the jar down to him. As he filled it with cool, clear water, she looked at his beautiful scales. In the bright sun of equatorial Africa, his scales scattered the sunlight into all directions in all the colors of the rainbows seen in rainy season.

Each day the girl went to the river, and on the seventh day, as the fish filled the jar, he looked up and into her eyes. She had grown to like the fish very much. His voice was pleasant, his scales were beautiful, and he was very kind. She bent low and allowed the fish to kiss her. Instead of being cold, as she had feared, the fish was warm and gentle. She embraced the fish, and she became his bride.

The girl's family had been very happy to get the clear water, but like the other villagers, they had wondered where she found it. And on this seventh day, her father had sent one of her younger brothers to follow the girl to the riverbed. The brother saw his sister bend down and kiss the fish. He ran back to the village to tell their father.

The family was angry that their daughter had married a fish, for this meant that there would be no wedding or exchange of gifts, and the rest of the village would consider the girl an outcast. They might also treat the girl's family as outcasts because they had a fish for an in-law.

The next day, the father would not allow the girl to go to the riverbed. Instead, the oldest brother went, carrying the water jar the way a woman would. When the brother stood in the mud with the water jar, the fish came up, thinking the shadow he saw on the mud was the shadow of his wife. The brother took out a sharp knife and killed the fish.

The brother brought the fish back and gave it to his father. The father believed that the fish might be an evil spirit, but he saw that it was dead, and threw it at the feet of his daughter. She took the fish in her arms and began to cry. She walked out of the hut carrying the body of her husband. No one tried to stop her, now that the fish was dead.

She walked back to the riverbed and stood in the mud, crying. Her tears hit the mud, and the river began to fill. As her tears fell, the river rose and flowed past her. As the water rose, the fish in her hands sank below the water. Her white dress billowed up around her in the current. The water rose above her head, and she joined her husband in water and in death.

But as she died, she and her white dress turned into a water lily. As a water lily, she had the most beautiful children, thousands of them, who spread along the river and remember her to this day.

The Sizimweh

This story is retold from the folklore of one of the groups of Tonga-speaking people of Zimbabwe.

A group of girls went down to the river to fish with their fish baskets. A young boy, who had no duties around his home that day, followed them, for many of them were friends of his older sister. Although the girls usually tolerated the boy's presence, today they told him to go back to the village and leave them alone. They went on down the path and along the river, trying to get away from the lonely boy. Each time they stopped to fish, they saw him following them .

They went further from the village than they had ever gone before, and stepped out into the shallow river and began to catch fish. The boy came and sat on the riverbank and watched them. After a few minutes, a storm blew in and heavy rain began to fall. The girls ran toward the opposite bank, away from the direction of the blowing rain. The boy stood and waved his arms at them.

"Don't go to that side of the river," he called. "The Sizimweh lives over there!"

The girls paid no attention, for they did not believe in the Sizimweh, the beast who comes and kills by night and can eat many cattle or people at one sitting. The girls took shelter under a large tree and laughed at the boy and the rain. The boy swam across the river and sat with them.

When the rain stopped, the girls were curious, and began to walk away from the river along a wide pathway. The boy looked at the path and said, "See how wide this path is. It was not made by men, but by a beast!" The girls only laughed and walked on.

They came to a great hut with a wide doorway.

The boy said, "See how wide this doorway is? It was not made for men, but for a beast!" The girls laughed and walked to the door and called. No one answered, and the girls went in. The great hut was decorated with the skins of every animal, and skulls and horns hung from every wall.

The boy said, "See the big game here? They were were not hunted by men, but by a beast!"

The girls were impressed, but they thought that the hut was that of a great warrior, and imagined marrying such a man. They built a fire, cooked the fish, and ate supper.

When the girls fell asleep, the boy shut the door to the great hut. He slept just inside it. In the middle of the night, the Sizimweh came home and found his door shut. Even the Sizimweh obeys the polite customs, so he called for whoever was inside to open the door. The boy refused to open the door.

The Sizimweh pushed the door over and stepped in. He sniffed the air with huge sniffs, drooled at the smell of humans, and said, in a voice like the growl of a lion, "Let me have one of these girls to eat!"

"No," said the brave boy. "These are my people and you will not eat them." The beast snorted, but backed out the doorway politely.

When the sun came up and the girls awoke, the boy asked, "Did you not hear him? Did you not see him? The Sizimweh came at midnight!" The girls laughed and said the boy had dreamed it all.

The girls went down to the river to fish, and the boy went to the trees and cut a trunk to carve a drum. Instead of going home that night, the girls went back to the great hut with the skulls and horns, still hoping to meet a great warrior. They cooked their fish and the boy brought in the drum he had carved. He took a skin off the wall and made the drumhead.

That night the girls slept on mats as before. The boy put the door back in its frame and shut it. He slept on the dirt just inside the door.

At midnight the Sizimweh came home and found the door shut. He called for the boy to open the door. The boy again refused to open the door, and sang and played his drum as his answer. The drum woke the girls, who lay very still. The Sizimweh pushed the door over and stepped in. He sniffed the air with huge sniffs and drooled at the smell of human beings.

The beast spoke, in a voice like the low call of an elephant. "Let me have one of these girls to eat!"

"No," said the brave boy. "These are my people and you will not eat them."

The beast snarled, but backed out politely.

When the sun came up, the boy asked, "Did you not hear him? Did you not see him?"

The girls answered that they had heard him and seen him. The boy told the girls to hide in the drum. The girls made themselves small, and got in the drum to hide. The boy left, carrying the drum with him.

The Sizimweh came back to the great hut as the sun rose, and with him came his many meat-eating friends: lions, wild dogs, leopards, and hyenas. They walked all around the hut, sniffing. All they could smell was the fish cooked the night before. They accused the Sizimweh of being mistaken, and of having smelled fish instead of human beings.

Then the hyenas found the tracks of the boy, and the beasts all went out and tracked him to the river. They overtook him and asked where all the girls were.

"There are no girls here, just me and my drum," said the boy. He began to play the drum, and the girls inside sang a pretty song. All the animals stood up on their back legs and began to dance. After the dance, the animals thanked the boy for playing for them. Then they turned on the Sizimweh and called him a liar. They killed him and tore his flesh and ate him.

The boy ran to the river and held the heavy drum over his head as he waded across. Back at the village, the girls came out of the drum and made themselves their true sizes again. They all thanked the boy. And after that, when the boy played his drum all the village came to listen and sing and dance, and the girls never tried to chase the boy away again.

Wild Man

Retold from Southern folklore and inspired by the stories of Aunt Hattie, this story is probably from the Tonga-speaking people of Zimbabwe, where killing cattle with a hot iron rod was a common practice among thieves—who would then offer to buy the meat of the mysteriously dead cow. It is told in Mississippi and other parts of the American South.

Mandy and John Junior were almost the same age and got along pretty well, considering that they were brother and sister. Their mother had made some fried pies and wanted to send some over to their aunt's house on the other side of the big marshy river. There were two bridges over that river: the wide, paved highway bridge and a little wooden footbridge way on down the river.

As she wrapped the pies in a dish towel and put them in a bucket, their mother said, "Take these fried pies over to Aunt Sarah's house, and don't stay and play all day, either." As Junior and Mandy were stepping off the porch, carrying the bucket between them, their mother added, "And go on the hard road, don't go down on the path through the marsh!" Then she smiled and waved goodbye.

Junior and Mandy had gone about a quarter-mile down the blacktop road when they laughed and decided to take the shortcut. Off the roadbed they went, and down into the marsh along the path the fishermen took. They were walking along, singing a song and swinging the bucket between them when they came to the footbridge. Some of the boards on the footbridge were rotten, and as they started across it the boards broke through. The two kids jumped back off the footbridge and scrambled to the bank.

"We can't get across here," Mandy said.

"Let's go on downstream to where the river widens out and gets shallow," said Junior.

Instead of going back to the hard road, and getting to Aunt Sarah's late, they went downstream. The river widened out and became shallow, and they tried to wade across. Out in the marsh they got lost.

They wandered about, and then they sat down and ate a pie.

"We're in trouble now," said Mandy. "We're out in the marsh. This is where the Wild Man lives."

"Ain't no such thing as the Wild Man," said Junior.

"Yes, there is," she answered, "and he steals cattle and he probably kills lost children, too."

"Ain't no such thing," said Junior.

They got up and started walking again, and came to an old, two-story house. They went up on the porch and knocked on the door to ask directions. A man came to the door and invited them in. He was very kind and smiled, and the kids went in.

"Sit down, children, and we'll have supper," he said. The two sat down at the table, but started getting a little worried when the man locked the door.

"I get scared at night," the man explained, "so I lock the door to keep the Wild Man out." He went to his kitchen and brought out big steaks he had been cooking on the stove, almost as if he'd known they were coming. They ate and ate; that man sure had a lot of beef.

When the kids thanked the man for the supper and said they had better start back home, he wouldn't let them go. "Oh, no, children," he said, "you must stay the night here, where you'll be safe. If you go out in the marsh and it gets dark, the Wild Man might get you."

The man showed the children, who were very worried by now, upstairs to a bedroom with a big mattress with lots of quilts on the floor.

"I live alone," said the man, "so I only have my one bed. You can sleep on this old mattress, though."

The kids thanked him and he said goodnight and shut the door. They heard the key turn in the lock.

"This is the Wild Man!" said Mandy suddenly, in a whisper. "We've been trapped by the Wild Man."

"Maybe there is such a thing after all," said Junior. He got down on the floor and looked for a crack between the floorboards. He found one and saw the man heating a long iron rod over the fire in his kitchen.

"There is such a thing after all!" said Junior. "He's heating up a hot iron rod. That's how he kills cattle without people knowing it!"

Mandy put her finger over her lips to say "be quiet," and the two kids tiptoed slowly and quietly to the window. They slowly opened the window and were climbing very slowly out, when the man downstairs listened, and heard nobody moving around upstairs. As Mandy set her foot quietly onto the tin roof, the man downstairs walked slowly over to the spot directly under the mattress. As Junior put his foot slowly onto the tin roof, the man raised the hot iron rod and pushed it against the ceiling.

The kids looked back and saw the hot iron rod burn up through the mattress where they would have been lying. Then they jumped off the low roof and landed in the high marsh grass with a splash. They ran and ran and ran. They finally hit the fishing path and ran along it to the footbridge.

Back at the two-story house, the man opened the door to the bedroom. There was the mattress with two holes burned it, but there were no kids. Seeing the open window, the man knew what had happened. He ran downstairs and unlocked the front door. He ran out into the night to try and catch Junior and Mandy. He followed them through the marsh, running a lot faster than they could.

At the footbridge, they didn't know what to do. Should they try to cross the bridge and go on to Aunt Sarah's, which was closer, or go back along the fishing path to the roadbed and toward home? Just then, they saw the Wild Man coming through the high grass.

"Let's cross the bridge," said Mandy. "We'll step over the missing boards. It's dark and he won't see how the bridge is falling in."

Mandy and Junior walked out onto the footbridge, and stepped very carefully over the holes as they crossed. The Wild Man saw them and came running toward the bridge. He ran out onto the footbridge and fell through into the deep part of the river.

Mandy and Junior ran all the way to Aunt Sarah's house and told what they had seen. The Wild Man was never heard of again, and no cattle were missing for a long time after that.

The Girl and the Ghost

This story may be from the Ibo-speaking people of Africa. It is told in Arkansas, Louisiana, Mississippi, and other parts of the American South, from whose folklore it is retold here.

Once there was an old man who had saved his money all his life, but his wife died, and then he didn't feel like living any more himself. At first he thought about leaving all the money to his only son and daughter-in-law. But after the old man's wife died, the son and the daughter-in-law were mean to him, so the old man decided to bury his silver dollars in three Mason jars under the tree by the well, and not give them to anyone just yet.

But the old man died before he could figure out who to give all his money to. The son and his wife left the old man's house empty and falling to ruin because they had a house of their own just down the lane from it. Only once did the son and his wife go into the old house, and when they did, a deep voice called down the chimney and said, "I'm going to jump!"

Knowing the voice of his dead father, the son ran out of the house with his wife right behind him. They never went back.

Now, their house, and the old house right beside it, were way out in the country. So every once in a while someone would stop by, traveling from one town to another, and ask for permission to spend the night. The son and his wife weren't nice to folks, so they would send the travelers down to the old house where the ghost would scare them away.

One evening a young girl came down the lane, traveling all alone because her old grandfather was sick at home. She was on her way to her only aunt's house, a long ways off, to get some help. She stopped at the son's house and asked if she could spend the night. The wife came to the door and felt sorry for the girl, so she gave her an iron skillet with some fried okra in it for supper, but she still sent her down to the old haunted house to sleep. The girl thanked the woman and went on down the lane.

The young girl went up and knocked on the door politely, and when no one answered she went in. She had a match in her apron, so she lit a fire in the fireplace and went outside quickly to pick up some more wood to stoke the fire. She set the skillet on two bricks at the edge of the fire and sat back to wait for her supper to heat. As she was sitting by the fire, she heard the deep voice come down the chimney.

"I'm going to jump!"

The girl sat there for a minute. "Go ahead and jump, then," she said. Nothing happened. The skillet began to sizzle.

A few minutes later she heard the voice, a little further down the chimney, say, "I'm going to jump!"

The girl didn't move. She sat there for a moment and said, "Go ahead and jump, then." Nothing happened.

A few minutes later the voice was in the chimney just above the fire. "I'm going to jump!"

The girl was sitting on her heels with her arms folded. She didn't move an inch. "Well, go ahead and jump, then."

A big, dark shape jumped out of the fireplace, but it didn't bother the girl. It sat in the corner the same way she was sitting, on its heels with its arms folded.

"You're welcome to eat supper with me," said the girl, who was afraid to look. The thing didn't answer.

A little while later, the supper was just about warm, and she said, "You're welcome to eat supper with me."

The thing didn't answer, and she didn't look at it.

A few minutes later the supper was hot, and she said, "Well, you're welcome to eat supper with me and if you don't want to, you can't say I didn't ask!" With that she ate her supper and walked over and climbed onto the old broken-down bed.

"You're welcome to share this old bed with me," said the girl, because she and her grandfather had to share the bed at their house. The thing still didn't answer, and she still didn't look at it.

After a minute or two, she said, "You're welcome to share this old bed with me." The thing didn't answer. She wasn't even sure it was still there, but she didn't look.

After another minute or two she said, "Well, you're welcome to share this old bed with me, but if you don't want to, you can't say I didn't ask." The fire died low and the young girl tried to sleep.

In the dark, the thing got up slowly and walked over to the foot of the bed. It took hold of the covers and began to slowly pull the old quilt off the girl.

"Stop that!" said the girl. "I'm tired and I need to rest."

The thing let go of the quilt and the girl pulled it back up over her shoulders. A moment later the thing took hold of the covers again and began to pull them off the girl.

"Now, stop that!" said the girl. "I'm too tired to play silly games. Go to sleep!"

The thing quit pulling the covers and the girl pulled the quilt back up over herself. Sure enough, a minute later the thing took hold of the covers and began to pull again.

"Well, I told you to stop that!" said the girl, sitting up. "What do you want, anyway?"

"Come with me," said the thing, in a deep voice. "I have something to show you. This is for you, your grandfather, and my son."

The girl got up and went outside, following the dark shape. It was the size of a man and it walked like her grandfather walked, but it didn't have any clothes or a face. The girl followed the thing to a tree by the well. The thing reached inside itself and pulled out three of its old bones. It stuck the bones in the ground.

"Dig here," it said, and it melted into a pool like fat in a hot skillet. The black pool soaked into the ground and was gone.

The next morning the girl awoke before dawn, and dug up the three Mason jars full of silver dollars. She went to the son's house and left the skillet and a jar of money on the porch. She filled the three holes in and took the bones to the graveyard.

She took two jars of money and went back home.

The thing was never seen again.

A year later the girl and her grandfather bought the old house and moved in, and they were very nice to their neighbors, even though their neighbors weren't very friendly to them—or anybody else, for that matter.

Wham! Slam! Jenny-Mo-Jam!

Although stories like this are told by many people of Africa, this one is not identified with any one language group. It is told in Texas and other parts of the American South, with many different versions that kids love. Here it is as told by Aunt Hattie.

Once there was a little boy and a little girl whose mother knew some magic spells; she had even taught them a few. As the two grew older, people told them that their grandmother was an evil witch who had a magic ball she used to hunt down children. The brother and sister wondered if these scary stories could be true. They begged their mother to let them go through the forest to the home of the old woman who had raised her.

"No, dear children," said their mother, "you must not go there. No one who has spent the night in that forest has ever returned!" The children assured their mother that no harm would come to them because

they also knew some magic spells and would be sure to be back home before it got dark.

Finally, the boy put his twelve dogs in their pen and told his mother that if anything happened to him and his sister he would give a special whistle that only the dogs could hear. If the mother heard the dogs barking for no apparent reason, she should let them out of the pen so they could run to the rescue. The children kissed their mother goodbye and left.

It was still early afternoon when the children started out for the grandmother's house in the forest, and after a long walk they found her working in her garden. All her plants were very tall and of very strange shapes and colors. When the old woman saw the children, she clapped her hands with glee and asked them their names.

"I'm Jenny," said the girl.

"I'm Mo," said the boy.

The old woman asked them to come inside and meet her own two children who were about the same size and age as Jenny and Mo, but whose ears were just a little bit too pointed and furry, and whose teeth were just a little bit too long and sharp.

The children played in the yard, but the old woman's kids didn't seem to know any of the right games. The children talked to the old woman and were surprised to see the sun suddenly go down. They had not realized how late it was. All too soon it was dark, and they had to stay the night in the old woman's house.

The grandmother told all four children to eat the corn pone that was on the table and to go upstairs and

get ready for bed. In the meantime, she set a great iron
kettle on the hearth and built a fire underneath it. She
filled the kettle with water and soon it began to boil.
Then the old woman went upstairs and showed the
children where to sleep. To her own children she gave
a dark bedsheet to sleep under; to Jenny and Mo she
gave a white bedsheet. Pretty soon the two wild-looking kids were asleep and snoring in a grunting sort of
way. Even Jenny fell asleep. But Mo was worried and
stayed awake.

Downstairs the old woman took a sharp knife out
of her belt and began to sharpen it on a whetstone.
Skreeetch ... skreeetch ... went the knife.

The witch called up to the children, "Are you
asleep yet?"

"Not me," said Mo. "When I'm at home and I can't
sleep my mother gives me the fiddle to play."

The old woman brought up a fiddle and the boy
sat on the floor and played and played. The witch sat
at the foot of the stairs, on the bottom step, and
sharpened her knife some more.

Skreeetch ... skreeetch.

The boy played the sweetest tune he knew, one
that his mother sometimes sang to him and his sister
to put them to sleep. Soon he heard the old witch
herself snoring at the bottom of the stairs.

The boy put down the fiddle and woke Jenny.
They fluffed up their feather pillows and laid them on
the pallet where they had been supposed to sleep, to
make it look like they were still there. Then they traded
the bedsheets so that the white sheet was over the
wild-looking kids. Jenny and Mo tiptoed down the

stairs past the sleeping witch and ran down the dark moonlit path toward their own home.

Pretty soon, the witch awoke. She went upstairs and over to the white sheet. She stabbed the children under it. When she lit a candle and saw that she had killed her own children, she was howling mad. She ran to her trunk and got out the magic glass ball. She flew down the stairs and out the front door. She rolled the magic ball down one path. It rolled away, but came rolling back after a few minutes. She knew they had not gone that way.

She rolled the ball down another path, and this time it kept going. She began to follow it, carrying with her a large ax from her shed.

Jenny and Mo heard the magic glass ball rumbling behind them like distant thunder. They knew what that sound must mean! They climbed a catalpa tree, and Mo gave the whistle that only his dogs could hear. Back at their house, the dogs began to bark and bark. The mother came out and turned the dogs loose.

Soon the magic ball rolled to a stop at the foot of the catalpa tree, and the witch came running after it with her ax. She began chopping down the tree, chanting, "Wham! Slam! Jenny-Mo-Jam! Wham! Slam! Jenny-Mo-Jam!" The chips of wood flew as the ax cut into the trunk of the tree.

Every time she sang her chant, Mo sang another spell: "Catalpa tree, when the ax goes 'chop,' grow big at the bottom, grow little at the top!" Every time a chip fell, another one grew back.

"Wham! Slam! Jenny-Mo-Jam! Wham! Slam! Jenny-Mo-Jam!"

"Catalpa tree, when the ax goes 'chop,' grow big at the bottom, grow little at the top!"

The catalpa tree stood firm.

It wasn't too long before those twelve dogs came running to help. They barked, jumped around, and bit the old witch. She swung her ax with one hand and her knife with the other. She killed eleven of the dogs, but the last dog jumped at her throat and sank his teeth in and killed her.

When Jenny and Mo climbed down, they took the big knife and cut out the witch's heart. They rubbed the heart on the noses of the dead dogs, and they all jumped back to life. The dogs and the kids walked home and met their mother just as the sun was coming up.

Wylie and the Hairy Man

The origin of this story is not identified with any one language group. It is told in North and South Carolina, Georgia, Florida, Alabama, Mississippi, Louisiana, and parts of Arkansas and Texas. The best-loved story about a young hero in the American South, it is retold here from folklore and inspired by the stories of Jackie Torrence.

Deep in the swamp, a boy named Wylie lived with his mama, who knew magic spells and secret charms. Wylie loved his mama, and his mama loved Wylie. Wylie's papa was dead and gone. He'd been killed many years before in a fight with the Hairy Man who lived in the swamp. The Hairy Man knew magic, too, but all his spells were bad spells. The Hairy Man knew secret charms, too, but all his charms were evil charms.

Everyone was afraid of the Hairy Man, but he never left the swamp. The Hairy Man himself wasn't afraid of anything—except dogs. That old Hairy Man sure didn't like dogs. So whenever Wylie went into the swamp to gather wood or pick berries, he would take his dogs along to protect him.

One day Wylie's mama sent him into the swamp to gather wood, but she told him to tie up his dogs first. He wasn't going very far from the shack, and if he took his dogs he would just play and play and be gone longer. The dogs would end up chasing rabbits and Wylie and the dogs would just play, and the wood gathering wouldn't get done. So she told him to tie up the dogs.

"See this here glass of milk?" she asked. "I put a spell on it. If that old Hairy Man starts to bother you, this milk will turn as red as blood and I'll set your dogs loose. That way you'll get the work done, but you'll still be safe."

Wylie set out to get wood for the supper fire. He wandered further and further from the shack, looking for dry wood for the fire. He got so far into the swamp that the Hairy Man smelled him coming, and when Wylie looked up from picking up a piece of wood, there he stood! That old Hairy Man!

"Hellooo, Wyyylie," said the Hairy Man. His voice sounded like Wylie's mama's meat grinder. "How are youuu?"

"I'm fine, Mr. Hairy Man," Wylie said with a gulp. "How are you?" Wylie began to back away.

"I'm huuungry," said the Hairy Man, moving toward Wylie.

"What've you got in mind to eat, Mr. Hairy Man?" asked Wylie, backing away further.

"Youuu," said the Hairy Man, moving closer.

Back at the shack, the glass of milk on the table turned as red as blood. Wylie's mama knew that Wylie was in trouble and she set the dogs loose. The dogs could smell that old Hairy Man, and they ran into the swamp, barking.

"What's that noooise?" asked the Hairy Man.

"Them are my dogs, Mr. Hairy Man," said Wylie.

"Wyyylie ... " said the Hairy Man, " ... good-byyye!"

The dogs came crashing through the underbrush and chased that old Hairy Man about a hundred miles. Wylie went home with the firewood, whistling all the way.

On another day, Wylie's mama sent him out into the swamp to pick berries. He tied up his dogs like she told him, so they wouldn't follow him. His mama put another glass of milk out on the table, with a spell on it. Wylie went to pick berries, carrying a big bucket. Wylie wandered further and further from the shack, looking for berry canes with ripe berries on them. He got so far into the swamp that the Hairy Man smelled him coming. When Wylie looked up from a cane of ripe berries, there he stood! That old Hairy Man!

"Hellooo, Wyyylie," said the Hairy Man. His voice sounded like claws scratching on a screen door. "Whaaat's new?"

"Not much, Mr. Hairy Man," said Wylie, backing away. "What's new with you?"

Back at the shack that glass of milk with the magic spell on it turned as red as blood, but Wylie's mama was outside beating the rugs. She didn't see the milk, so she didn't set the dogs loose.

"I'm still huuungry," said the Hairy Man, coming closer to Wylie.

"Want some berries?" asked Wylie, throwing the bucket at the Hairy Man.

"No, thaaanks," said the Hairy Man, batting the bucket aside. "I've got something biiigger in mind."

Wylie climbed a cypress tree and the Hairy Man came slowly over to the knees at the bottom of the tree. He looked up at Wylie.

"I'm going to eat youuu, Wyyylie," said the Hairy Man.

Now, those dogs ought to have been there by then, but Wylie couldn't hear them barking.

"Before you eat me, Mr. Hairy Man … "

"Yesss, Wyyylie … "

"Before you eat me, would you show me how good you can do magic spells?"

The Hairy Man puffed out his chest and acted real proud at that. "Suuure, Wyyylie," said the old Hairy Man. "What shall I dooo?"

"Well, sir," said Wylie, "could you make a big bunch of rope just appear out of nowhere?"

"Suuure," said the Hairy Man, standing at the foot of the cypress tree. "Rope, rope, lots of rooope!" yelled the Hairy Man. And suddenly there were ropes hanging all over the trees and piled all around on the ground.

"Now I can get away," yelled Wylie up in the tree. He started to grab a rope like he was going to swing from one tree to another to escape. "You'd have to make all the rope in the swamp vanish to catch me now!"

"Aaall the rope in the swaaamp," growled the Hairy Man, "vaaanish!"

All the rope on the ground vanished. All the rope in the trees vanished. The rope holding up Wylie's pants vanished, and he nearly lost his pants.

All the rope tying up his dogs vanished, too, and they came crashing through the underbrush, barking and howling.

"Wyyylie," said the Hairy Man, "goodbyyye!"

And those dogs chased that old Hairy Man about two hundred miles through the swamp.

Wylie held up his pants with one hand and carried the bucket in the other hand as he walked back home.

After that day, no matter how long it took to run his errands in the swamp, no matter how much those dogs played and played, and no matter how late Wylie came in from his chores at night, Wylie's mama didn't ever make him tie up those dogs again!

Animal Fables

In the African cultures, talking animal stories are told to, by, and for all age groups. They teach proper behavior to children, reinforce it in older people, entertain everyone, and keep family and community bonds strong.

In these stories, called animal fables, the animals not only act like animals, they also act like human beings. There is always a gentle lesson somewhere in the tale, something important about human relationships and behavior taught without mentioning any specific person or even people in general.

Among some language groups of Africa, the meanings of names used for family members are different from the English ones. Any man or woman in the same generation as your father and mother would be addressed as "Uncle" or "Aunt." Anyone of your same generation would be addressed by you as "Sister" or "Brother." This polite kinship system appears in many animal fables, too. It is a way of showing and teaching respect for all of our fellow beings, both the human ones and the animal ones.

Python and Lizard

Retold from folklore and inspired by the stories of Lloyd Wilson, this story was not told in America until recently, because the two animals in it are not found in America. It is told by the Baganda-speaking people of Uganda.

In the land of the Baganda, on Lake Victoria, was a village in the ancient times, wherein lived the ancestors of the animals of today. When it was a feast day, the best singer at their dance was the lizard. The best dancer was the python. All the animals in the village admired Lizard and Python, and soon there was talk of a challenge between them. But Lizard and Python were close friends, and besides, Lizard always acknowledged Python as the better dancer, and Python never failed to mention that Lizard was the better singer.

When it came to playing the drum, the two friends were more evenly matched. Some of the animals took sides as to which of the two friends was the better drummer.

Drums were very rare in the ancient times, and Lizard did not own a drum of his own. But Python owned a fine drum, and always let Lizard borrow it whenever he wanted. Because good drums were hard to get in those days, Python would not loan his drum to anyone but his friend Lizard.

One day there was a feast being given by the chieftain of the village, and he invited Lizard to sing, and Python to dance, and both of them to play the drum for the honored guest, the chief of another village across the lake. Lizard played the drum while Python danced, and Python played the drum while Lizard sang. The visiting chief was very impressed, and not knowing to whom the drum belonged, he invited Lizard to come and sing at the next feast in the distant village. The visiting chief told Lizard to bring his drum, not thinking that the drum might not belong to him.

Python was not present when Lizard was called into the chief's hut to receive the invitation, so he did not know about it. Needing a drum, and knowing that Python would not let his drum leave the village for fear something might happen to it, Lizard decided to lie to his old friend. Lizard asked to borrow the drum for three days to practice playing on it. Python thought about it a while, and then agreed to let Lizard borrow the drum.

Lizard took the drum and went across to the other village and played and sang at their feast. His music was so popular with the animals of the other village that he completely forgot his agreement with Python to return the drum after three days. Lizard stayed day after day in the other village, playing at the request of the other chief. That chief had his own group of musicians in his compound of huts, and Lizard sang and played Python's drum as the other musicians played their violins and bowl-lyres. The chief loved it, and rewarded Lizard well for his performances.

Back home, four days passed and Lizard had not returned the drum. Python went to Lizard's hut to ask for the drum, but Lizard was not there. Lizard's wife told Python the truth, for she was good friends with Python's wife. Python went home very disappointed with his old friend's unkind treatment.

When Lizard got home, carrying his gifts from the chief and his court across the lake, he was so full of self-praise that he decided the drum should belong to him, for he was more talented than Python anyway. When Python heard Lizard was back in their village, and went to Lizard's hut to get the drum, Lizard took the drum and ran out the rear doorway and over to a tall tree. He climbed the tree, knowing that Python could not climb after him.

Python coiled himself at the base of the tree and looked up at his old friend. Python told Lizard how wrong it had been of him to take the drum under false promise, and how poor a friend he was now. Lizard felt guilty, but to hide his guilt, he began to call out insults to his old friend. Lizard said he deserved the drum because he could play with his feet or his tail, while Python could only play the drum with his tail.

Python went sadly home, sorry to lose the drum, but much sorrier to lose the friendship of Lizard.

Lizard sat in the tree and sang loudly and played the drum until dark, to taunt Python. After dark, Lizard went home. Lizard's wife scolded him for being such a poor friend, and she threw a pot at him! Lizard took his drum and ran outside. She was right, of course, and Lizard knew it, but he wasn't going to step off the path he had started to walk, out of pride. He just went up another tree and sang and played until the moon came up.

Python went to the termite hill and asked to speak with the termite queen. She came out and they had a feast, and all her people watched as Python danced for them, and bowed very low before the termite queen. When she told him how much she admired and appreciated his dancing, she offered him a gift of his choosing. He asked that her people come with him to the tree where Lizard sat with the stolen drum. The termite queen sent her warriors in a long line behind Python, and they came to the tree wherein Lizard sat.

As Lizard taunted Python and called him names, the termite warriors ate and ate and ate at the tree. Soon Lizard and the drum came tumbling down into the river that ran below the tree.

The termite warriors returned to the termite hill as Python slid slowly into the water and swam toward Lizard. Lizard could not swim, and was thrashing about terribly. He saw Python coming, and feared that his death was near. Python rescued the drum from the water and set it on the ground, then he turned and slowly swam toward Lizard, staring straight into

Lizard's wide eyes as Lizard struggled and called for mercy.

Python slowly wrapped one end of himself around his old friend Lizard, and Lizard felt his death was nearer!

Slowly and without a word, Python wrapped his other end around the fallen tree and pulled his old friend to the shore. He dumped Lizard on the bank of the river, gasping for air and working his jaws. Even the gentlest grip of Python had been enough to squeeze Lizard's scrawny neck hard, and Lizard's cheeks puffed out and have never gone down to this day.

Python forgave his friend, and Lizard apologized—when he got his breath back—but their friendship was never the same again. Python never loans his drum to anyone, and stares mistrustfully at you if he does not know you. Lizard still has swollen cheeks, and works his jaw as if he still can't get his breath.

Before Lizard climbs a tree limb or a tall weed, he shakes it to see if there are termites in it.

And you never see a lizard in a tree playing a drum ... do you?

Mr. Frog Rides Mr. Elephant

Retold from folklore and inspired by the stories of Tyrone Wilkerson, this is a story from the people of Angola. It became "Mr. Rabbit Fools Mr. Fox" or "Brother Rabbit Tricks Brother Fox" in the American South.

Sitting along the riverbank, the frogs were talking. Mr. Frog began to brag about how important he was. "Hippopotamus is my personal servant," he claimed, lying, "and ... and ... Mr. Elephant is my personal riding-mount!"

All the little frogs laughed and showed that they didn't believe Mr. Frog. Miss Frog, who had no husband, seemed impressed and she said, "You may come to call at my house tomorrow, Mr. Frog. I hope you will come riding your personal riding-mount."

Mr. Frog realized he had bragged way too much, and he swallowed hard. "Gulp!" Then Miss Frog hopped home and the little frogs who had been listening laughed again and hopped away. Mr. Frog wondered how he could impress Miss Frog, whom he wanted to marry. "Gulp!" he said.

The next morning Mr. Elephant came to the river-bank to get a drink and the little frogs started laughing at him. "Peep, peep, peep!"

"What are you laughing at, little frogs?" said Mr. Elephant sternly.

"Mr. Frog said you were his personal riding-mount!" said the little frogs. "He told it to Miss Frog."

Mr. Elephant twitched his tail and flapped his big ears a little. "He did, did he?" he asked.

"He did! He did! He did!" peeped the little frogs.

"I'll teach him to mock me," said Mr. Elephant, turning and walking down the bank, swinging his trunk.

Mr. Frog saw Mr. Elephant coming and was afraid. "Gulp!" he said. Quickly, Mr. Frog flopped over on his back like he was dead. Mr. Elephant came right up to him and bumped him with his trunk.

"Get up, Mr. Frog," said Mr. Elephant.

"I can't, Mr. Elephant," said Mr. Frog. "I'm much too sick. I ate a bug that poisoned me. I'm dying!"

"Get up, Mr. Frog," said Mr. Elephant. "We're going to Miss Frog's house and you're going to set the record straight!"

"I'm too sick. I'm dying. Don't make me go!"

"Get up, Mr. Frog, and we'll go set the record straight before you die."

"I'm too sick; I can't hop."

"I'll carry you," said Mr. Elephant.

"You'll drop me," said Mr. Frog. "I couldn't go unless I rode upon your neck."

"I'll pick you up and put you on my neck!" said Mr. Elephant, impatiently.

"I'm too sick—I'd fall off. I couldn't ride you without a howdah, a riding-seat like Mr. Camel wears," said Mr. Frog, still lying on his back.

"I'll make a howdah," said Mr. Elephant, and he went to the bush and pulled down a vine with a gourd on it. He hit the gourd against the trunk of a tree with his own trunk. The gourd broke in half and looked like a howdah. Mr. Elephant plodded back to the riverbank and tossed his trunk up and dropped the vine over his neck. Mr. Frog got up, very feebly, and tied the vine under Mr. Elephant's wrinkled chin. Then Mr. Elephant lifted Mr. Frog on his trunk and set him on his neck. Mr. Frog hopped merrily into the half-gourd howdah and sat up like a prince.

Mr. Elephant lumbered along the riverbank until he came to Miss Frog's house. Miss Frog looked out and saw Mr. Frog riding high and proud in the half-gourd howdah. She was very impressed.

"Hold it, Mr. Elephant!" called Mr. Frog to his riding-mount. Mr. Elephant stopped. "Let me down," called Mr. Frog. Mr. Elephant lifted Mr. Frog out of the half-gourd howdah and lowered him to the ground. Mr. Frog hopped over into Miss Frog's house. Mr. Elephant stood outside, swaying from side to side, waiting.

Inside, Mr. Frog explained to Miss Frog that indeed he was a very prominent member of the riverbank community, and that indeed Mr. Elephant was his personal riding-mount. Than he asked Miss Frog to become his bride. She agreed. Mr. Frog said he would go home and return the following day.

He hopped back out and called, "Up, Mr. Elephant."

Mr. Elephant lifted him into the half-gourd howdah, and turned and walked slowly back along the riverbank. Mr. Frog turned and waved to Miss Frog, who watched him go with deep admiration.

Back at his house, Mr. Frog called to be put down.

"I told Miss Frog all about you and me. I set the record straight," he said, as he hopped off Mr. Elephant's trunk.

Mr. Elephant took the vine in his trunk, yanked it off, and threw it in the river.

"I'll just go inside and die now, Mr. Elephant," said Mr. Frog. "Goodbye."

"I hope you learned your lesson," said Mr. Elephant with a snort. Then he raised his trunk and trumpeted. He tramped off into the bush.

Mr. Frog took all his belongings and burned his house and started off for the village of Miss Frog's family, singing as he went.

Brother Lion and Brother Man

This story mixes the African lion, the American bear, and the trickster rabbit who may be the Tonga-speaking people's hare trickster. Because it centers so on the animals' hunt for man, instead of on a trick, it is included here. This story probably came from the west coast of Africa and is told throughout the South and West in America. It is presented here as retold from folklore by Tyrone Wilkerson.

Now the she-lion does most of the hunting, but the he-lion thinks of himself as the king of the beasts.

He thinks, "Me, myself, and I. That's all. That's the only king of beasts! Me, myself, and I!"

One day, old Mister Lion woke up, and looked around, and started in to roaring, "Me, myself, and I! Me, myself, and I!" All this roaring made the squirrels and the chipmunks and the other animals start looking for the next boat out of there. They didn't want to hang around and get eaten by a big-mouthed he-lion!

The bragging and boasting and roaring went on for several days, and the animals couldn't understand what had gotten into the old he-lion. He was stalking back and forth, parading around, being king of the beasts. The other animals were afraid to come out of their dens.

"We've got to do something about Mister Lion," said the small animals. "We can't go out and eat, and we can't send our children out, either. If we leave our dens and nests to eat, Mister Lion will be eating us instead!" The smaller animals went out the back doors of their dens and nests to find the two animals they thought could solve the problem. First, they went for Brother Rabbit because he was the sneakiest animal, and loved to play tricks on his neighbors. Then they went for Brother Bear, who had lived in the woods the longest, and knew what was what with all the animals who lived there.

The small animals gathered around Brother Bear and Brother Rabbit, who were sitting on stumps, drinking coffee, playing checkers, and cheating.

Brother Chipmunk said, "Brother Bear, Brother Rabbit, we got ourselves a problem."

"Well," said Brother Bear, "what is it?"

Brother Squirrel said, "It's old Mr. Lion. He's got to stalking all around the woods going, 'Me, myself, and I! Me, myself, and I!' He's got all us little guys scared to death."

Brother Rabbit laughed, "That's funny!"

Brother Bear said, "Hush up, Rabbit! These folks came to ask for our help, and here you are laughin' at 'em!"

Brother Rabbit came to his senses and got quiet and let Brother Bear speak.

"Okay, I tell you what. We'll go up the hollow and visit old Mister Lion and see if we can calm down this big cat, so you-all won't have to be scared all the time."

"Uh-uh!" said Brother Rabbit, shaking his head. "*You* can go see Mr. Lion if you want, but *we* ain't goin' anywhere. I'm staying put. That he-lion likes rabbit meat!"

Brother Bear got embarrassed at Brother Rabbit's fraidy-cat attitude, and he said, "You'll go with me and we'll talk to old Mr. Lion, or I'll sit right down on your head right now!"

Now, Brother Rabbit could imagine how he'd look all mashed out flat, with his long feet sticking out from under Brother Bear, so he right quick agreed to go along. The other animals thanked them, and stayed by the checkerboard while Brother Bear and Brother Rabbit went up the hollow, with Brother Rabbit spending considerable time right behind the widest part of Brother Bear's back.

When they found the old he-lion he was sleeping under a tree, batting flies off his nose with his tail, snoring in a growling way. Brother Rabbit looked out from behind Brother Bear and said, "Well, wake him up."

"Ahem," Brother Bear cleared his throat with a grunt. "Brother Lion, come on and wake up."

"Me, myself, and I!" He-Lion roared as he stood up and stretched. Brother Rabbit went from behind Brother Bear to behind the nearest tree.

"I've got something to ask you, Brother Lion," said Brother Bear.

Old He-Lion stood blinking and licking his chops. "Ask me," he said. "I'm the king of the beasts."

"Why are you parading around here saying, 'Me, myself, and I'? Don't you realize that you're not the biggest and baddest thing in the forest?"

Mister Lion stiffened and squinted at Brother Bear. "What do you mean, I'm not the biggest and baddest thing in the forest? I'm the *king* of the forest! Who's king if I'm not king?"

"Man is," said Bear.

"Man? Who's Man?" asked old He-Lion. "I've never seen Man before!"

Sure enough, old He-Lion had never seen a man before because, you see, Man hadn't made it that deep into the woods yet.

Lion roared, "Show me Man! I want to see Man!"

Brother Rabbit moved one tree further away from Brother Lion.

"All right," said Brother Bear, "come along, and we'll show you Man."

"We who?" snarled the old he-lion. "I don't see anybody but you."

Brother Rabbit sort of waved one paw around the tree and said feebly, "Morning, Mister Lion, sir."

Brother Bear and the old he-lion walked past Brother Rabbit, and the lion gave him a sideways glance. Brother Rabbit grinned his biggest, friendliest grin, and hopped in alongside Brother Bear, staying on the other side from old He-Lion. They went along the path until they came near the edge of the woods. There, in the path, they saw a young boy playing with a stick, hitting a rock along the road.

Now, old He-Lion had never seen anyone walk on two legs before, and he growled, "Oh, that's got to be him. That's got to be Man. That's him! That's him!" And he crept around the boy and came up behind him. "Me, myself, and I!" he roared at the boy.

The boy turned around and looked down the old lion's throat as he roared. "Mama!" the boy hollered, and ran away down the path.

Old He-Lion began to laugh; he laughed and laughed. "I told you Man was nothing! Look at him run, hollering for his mama!"

Brother Rabbit thought it was funny, too. He laughed and laughed. "That's a good one," he said. "Me, myself, and I … me, myself, and I!"

"You-all hush up," snapped Brother Bear. "That wasn't Man. That's *going to be* Man, but that wasn't Man. Come on, Brother Lion, we're going to show you Man, to prove who's king." Sure enough, they went down the road a little further, with the lion strutting proudly, twitching his tail, and they saw a man walking with a cane.

"Oh, now, that's got to be Man," said the old he-lion. "He's bigger than the other one!" And he stalked up behind that old fellow and roared, "Me, myself, and I!" The old man turned around and saw that lion, and he whopped him alongside of the head with his cane and ran down the road. Old He-Lion shook his head once and laughed. "I told you Man was nothing. Look how he's running down the road!" He laughed and laughed.

Brother Rabbit liked that, too. He laughed and laughed.

"No, no, no," said Brother Bear, "that wasn't Man either. That *used to be* Man, but that wasn't Man." They walked down the road a little further.

Now, there was a fine young man out bird hunting with a shotgun. If Mister Lion didn't know what Man was, he sure didn't know what a shotgun was. But Brother Rabbit did, and he laughed out loud. "There's Man," he called out to the old he-lion. "There he is; that's him. Go pull your tricks on him!"

"Ahem," said Brother Bear, clearing his throat with a snort, "I wouldn't do that if I were you." Brother Rabbit tried to hush up Brother Bear, but Mister Lion was already creeping up on the young man.

"ME, MYSELF, AND I!" he roared at the top of his lungs.

The young man turned around and said, "Oh, big game today!" He raised his shotgun and fired: boom!

Mister Lion shook himself once, and stretched out his neck to roar again, "Me, my ..."

Boom!

The old he-lion was starting to sting. He opened his mouth, "Me ..."

Boom! The young man had reloaded.

Mister Lion turned and ran.

Brother Rabbit laughed and laughed. "Well, Mister Lion, now you've met Man. You've met Man, and he's not what you think!"

As the three of them loped along back into the woods, the old he-lion snarled, "I don't like Mister

Man. He's got a stick that smokes and stings. I don't like Mister Man at all!"

Brother Bear said, "I guess you'll calm down from now on."

Brother Rabbit was running to keep up, and didn't have the breath to say anything at all.

The next morning the old he-lion woke up and yawned. He looked all around to see that Brother Bear wasn't anywhere near. He stood up and stretched. He opened his big old mouth and said, "Me ... myself ... and Man!"

How Br'er Rabbit Outsmarted the Frogs

This famous Southern animal fable was told to the editors at a storytelling festival. There are many versions of this story in folklore, but this one, as told by Jackie Torrence, is the best.

Back in the days when the animals could talk, there lived old Br'er Rabbit. He was a fine fisherman who could go down to the river, drop his line into the water, and inside of ten minutes he could have twenty-five fish resting right there on the bank beside him. But Br'er Rabbit's good friend Br'er Raccoon couldn't catch fish at all. And he didn't like fish, he liked frogs instead.

So Br'er 'Coon would go down to the river carrying a tow sack. He'd sneak up behind a frog, grab him, and drop him in the bag. When the sack was full, he'd go home, open the door, and there would be his wife, standing there waiting for him.

"Oh, good," she'd say. "You brought home a great big passel of frogs. I'm so happy!"

One day the frogs called a great big frog meeting because they were tired of some of them being caught by Br'er 'Coon. They all agreed they had to do something to keep the racoon from catching them. They decided to put a lookout frog on duty on the bank. They needed some frog with good eyes, good hearing, and a good, loud voice to warn them. They elected the bullfrog. The bullfrog would sit down on the bank and watch for Br'er 'Coon. When old Br'er 'Coon would get within about a half a mile of the river, the bullfrog would call out:

> Here he comes!
> Here he comes!
> Here he comes!

The little frogs along the river would peep:

... here he comes ... here he comes ... here he comes ....

When Br'er 'Coon arrived at the riverbank there wasn't a frog in sight, and he couldn't swim so he couldn't go after them. When he got home with that empty tow sack, there would be his wife, waiting for him.

"You done come home with an empty tow sack?" she would demand.

"Well, I can't catch them frogs," Br'er 'Coon would answer. "They is all too wild to catch. Every time I get within half a mile of that riverbank, every frog around yells, 'Here he comes, here he comes, here he comes!' And I can't catch a single frog!"

Well, that would make his wife mad and she'd pick up the broom and chase him all around the house. "We is all going to starve to death!" she hollered. "Get back down there and *catch them frogs!*"

One morning Br'er 'Coon left his house with a bump on his head and an empty tow sack, and as he was going down the road, he met Br'er Rabbit coming up the road. Br'er Rabbit had been fishing, and he had a string of fish hanging down his back.

"Well, howdy-do, Br'er 'Coon," said the rabbit. "How is you?"

"I ain't doing so good," said Br'er 'Coon.

"Well, you looks right down in the mouth," said the rabbit.

"It ain't my mouth that I'm down in," said Br'er 'Coon. "See this bump on my head? My wife gave that to me with her broomstick!"

"Well, why'd she do that?"

"I can't catch no frogs."

"Can't catch no frogs?" asked Br'er Rabbit. "Why, there's a thousand frogs down there at the river."

"But I can't catch 'em. I goes halfway to the river and all I can hear is, 'Here he comes, here he comes, here he comes!' By the time I get there, they is all in the water."

"Well, sir," said Br'er Rabbit, "you needs you a plan."

"I don't know nothing about planning," said Br'er 'Coon.

"Don't you worry," said Br'er Rabbit. "I'm the best planner that ever planned a plan. I've just got to sit here in the road for a while and think one up for you!" The rabbit sat back on his hind legs and put his ears up. First he scratched one ear with one hind leg, and then he scratched the other ear with the other hind leg. Then he hopped up and said, "I've got you a plan!"

"What is it?" asked Br'er 'Coon.

"Well, sir, come on over here. I don't want nobody to hear it." And they moved over closer to each other, and Br'er Rabbit looked all about, and said, "This here's your plan. Go on down to the river and when you gets there, fall down and play dead like Br'er 'Possum."

"Then what does I do?" asked Br'er 'Coon.

"You don't do nothing. Just lay there and don't move for nothing. Don't move till I tells you to move," said Br'er Rabbit.

"That's a wonderful plan," said Br'er 'Coon, walking toward the river. "I don't understand it, but it's a wonderful plan!"

Just as Br'er 'Coon got about a half-mile from the river, he could hear the bullfrogs start up:

> Heeeeere he comes!
> Heeeeere he comes!
> Heeeeere he comes!

And the little frogs peeped:

> ... here he comes ... here he comes ... here he comes ....

But Br'er 'Coon went on down to the river and there he commenced to dying. "Oooooh," he groaned, "I'm dying of starvation. I ain't had no frogs to eat for days and days. Ooooooh, I'm dead." And he fell on his back and stuck his feet straight up in the air and kicked about nine times. He lay there just like he was dead. Even when the sun came out and he commenced to sweat, he didn't move an inch.

Then the flies came in and landed on Br'er 'Coon. They walked all around on his tummy and all around his face and in and out his nose, and their little feet tickled and tickled, but he didn't move. The sun went on down and the flies went away in the evening breeze.

Along the trail came Br'er Rabbit, strutting up to the riverbank. He stopped at the sight of Br'er 'Coon, and, looking to see if the frogs had popped their eyes up above the water and were watching him, he commenced to crying. "Oooooo-hoooo-hoooo!" he cried. "My best friend, Old Br'er 'Coon, has done fell dead!"

The frogs all came crawling out of the water to take a look at the dead raccoon. The bullfrogs called:

> That be good!
> That be good!
> Thaaaaat be good!

And the little frogs peeped back:

> ... that be good ... that be good ... that be good ....

"Well, sir," said Br'er Rabbit, "I guess I'd better get to digging his grave. I promised him years ago I'd bury him when he passed on, and bury him here in his favorite place, right by this here river!"

And the bullfrogs said:

> Le-e-et us dig it!
> Le-e-et us dig it!
> Le-e-et us dig it!

And the little frogs peeped:

... let us dig it ... let us dig it ... let us dig it ....

"Well, sir," said Br'er Rabbit, "since I'm so tore up with grief and all, I guess I'll let you dig it. But I'd better stay here and tell you how deep to dig it."

So all the frogs went and got their frog shovels and got in a circle around Br'er 'Coon, who was just lying there playing dead. They started to dig, and they dug and they dug and they dug. Old Br'er 'Coon was going further and further down as the grave got deeper, and the frogs were going down with him.

When the grave was deep, the bullfrog jumped up on Br'er 'Coon's chest and yelled out of the grave to Br'er Rabbit:

> I-i-is it deep enough?
> I-i-is it deep enough?
> I-i-is it deep enough?

And the little frogs peeped:

... is it deep enough ... is it deep enough ... is it deep enough ....

"Well," said Br'er Rabbit, "can you jump out?"
The bullfrog looked up and said:

> Yes we can!
> Yes we can!
> Yes we can!

... yes we can ... yes we can ... yes we can ....

"Well, it ain't deep enough. Dig it deeper!" said Br'er Rabbit.

So the frogs dug, and they dug and they dug and they dug. When that grave was twelve feet deep, and Old Br'er 'Coon was just lying there, the bullfrog thought that was deep enough, so he hopped up on Br'er 'Coon's chest and yelled up out of the grave:

> I-i-is it deep enough?
> I-i-is it deep enough?
> I-i-is it deep enough?

… is it deep enough … is it deep enough … is it deep enough ….

Br'er Rabbit said, "Well, can you jump out?"
And the frogs looked up and the bullfrog said:

> Belie-e-ve we can.
> Belie-e-ve we can.
> Belie-e-ve we can.

… believe we can … believe we can … believe we can ….

"Well, it ain't deep enough," said Br'er Rabbit. "Dig it deeper."

And the frogs kept digging, and they dug and they dug and they dug.

That grave was fifteen feet deep, and the shovelfuls of dirt that they threw upward fell right back down on their heads. And the bullfrog just kind of climbed up on Br'er 'Coon's chest and yelled up out of the grave:

> I-i-is it deep enough?
> I-i-is it deep enough?
> I-i-is it deep enough?

… is it deep enough … is it deep enough … is it deep enough ….

"Well," said Br'er Rabbit, "can you jump out?"
And the bullfrog looked up, and looked and looked, and said:

> No-o-o we can't.
> No-o-o we can't.
> No-o-o we can't.

... no we can't ... no we can't ... no we can't ....

Br'er Rabbit yelled down to Br'er 'Coon, "Get up there, Br'er 'Coon. Pick up your groceries. The grave is too deep to jump out of."

So, Br'er 'Coon jumped up and started grabbing frogs and throwing them into that tow sack. Well, Br'er 'Coon had so many frogs he had enough to eat for this year and the next year to boot!

And that's the end of that!

Trickster Stories

The trickster is the most beloved character in stories all around the world. To the people of Africa, the trickster is Anansi the Spider among the Ashanti, Ijapa the Tortoise among the Yoruba-speaking people, Munsanje the Hare among Tonga-speaking people, and the Hare or the Chevrotain—similar to a deer—among the Mbundu-speaking people.

People love the trickster because he is the "little guy" who gets the better of bigger opponents. We do not always like what the trickster does, for he is often silly, greedy, and selfish, but we do admire his childlike charm and quick wit. Though he is often lazy, the trickster also shows how human beings must be constantly on guard against the things that can happen in nature—like floods or storms or fires.

Sometimes the trickster is the character who takes fire from nature and gives it to the people, or he does some other good deed to "trick" nature or an evil spirit and help the people. Then the people are willing to forgive the trickster for his childish little pranks out of gratitude to him for his good deed of long ago.

Anansi Tries to Steal All the Wisdom in the World

This story is retold from folklore based on the stories of Len Cabral. It begins with the statement, "We do not really mean it ..." used by some of the Ashanti people to tell listeners that the story is not part of their history.

We do not really mean it. We do not really mean it, but they say:

Anansi, the spider, knew that he was not wise. He was clever, but not wise. He thought, "If I can get all the wisdom in the world and put it in a gourd, then I will be very wise when compared to everyone else."

He went around from village to village, carrying a gourd. He asked everyone to put some of their wisdom in the gourd. They laughed, but each gave Anansi some wisdom, knowing he could certainly use it! Soon he had a whole gourd full of wisdom.

Anansi tried to think where to put this wisdom so that no one else could use it, making him seem wise by comparison. He looked up a tall tree and decided to put the gourd up there where no one could find it.

Anansi took a cloth band and tied it around his waist and put the gourd in the band in front of his stomach. He began to try to climb the tree. But the gourd full of wisdom got in his way. He could not climb, though he tried and tried.

Along came Anansi's youngest son.

"Father, what are you doing?"

"I am climbing this tree with this gourd full of wisdom."

"Father, it would be better if you put the gourd behind you in the band instead of in front."

Anansi stood there quietly for a long time, and then he said, "Shouldn't you be going home now?"

The young spider went home. Anansi moved the gourd in the band at his waist. This time he put it behind him. He climbed the tree.

From the top of the tree he spoke aloud, "I collected a whole gourd full of wisdom, and my baby son is still wiser than I am! Take your wisdom back!"

Anansi cracked the gourd open and scattered the wisdom in the wind. The wisdom floated down everywhere. That is how everyone got wisdom.

And anyone who did not run there in time to pick some of the wisdom up is … forgive me for saying it … a fool.

This is my story. If it is sweet, or if it is not sweet, take it home with you. And let some of it come back to me.

Why Anansi has a Narrow Waist

This story, as told by Len Cabral, is one of the many Anansi stories from the Tshi-speaking Ashanti people of the region of the White Volta and Black Volta rivers on the western coast of Africa, just above the equator.

One day Anansi, the spider, was walking along when he suddenly smelled something delicious. He smelled greens cooking in someone's pot. Anansi loved greens! So he went into the village. The people saw him and they all loved Anansi, so they said, "Come, Anansi, sit down and tell us a story. When the greens are done, we'll have lunch!"

"Oh, well," said Anansi, who was sometimes rather lazy, "I have an errand to run. But I tell you what. I'll spin a web thread and give you one end of the string. I'll tie the other end around my waist. When the greens are done, just give a pull on that string, and I'll come join you for lunch."

And that's what he did. He left with the string tied around his waist and walked onto the road again. He went a little further and he smelled beans cooking. Anansi loved beans! So he went into the village. The people saw him and they all loved Anansi, so they said, "Come, Anansi, sit down and tell us a story. When the beans are done, we'll have lunch!"

"Oh, well," said Anansi, "I have an errand to run. But I tell you what. I'll spin a thread and give you one end of the string. I'll tie the other end around my waist. When the beans are done, just give a pull on that string, and I'll come join you for lunch."

And that's what he did. He left with the second string tied around his waist and walked onto the road again. He went a little further and he smelled yams cooking. Anansi loved yams! So he went into the village. The people saw him and they all loved Anansi, so they said, "Come, Anansi, sit down and tell us a story. When the yams are done, we'll have lunch!"

"Oh, well," said Anansi, "I have an errand to run. But I tell you what. I'll spin a thread and give you one end of the string. I'll tie the other end around my waist. When the yams are done, just give a pull on that string, and I'll come and join you for lunch."

And that's what he did.

Pretty soon, Anansi was sitting in the brush, waiting quietly with eight strings tied around his waist, waiting for one pot of lunch to get done. Just then, the people cooking greens tasted the greens, and they were just right. They pulled on the string and said, "Come, Anansi. Come, Anansi."

Anansi felt the pull and said, "Oh, greens, I love greens!"

He was about to go to that village, but just then, the people cooking beans tasted the beans, and they were just right. They pulled on their string and said, "Come, Anansi. Come, Anansi."

Anansi felt that pull and said, "Oh, beans, I love beans!" But now he was being pulled two ways.

Just then, the people cooking yams tasted the yams, and they were just right. They pulled on the string and said, "Come, Anansi. Come, Anansi."

Now Anansi was being pulled three ways at once. Just then, all the cooking pots were ready in all the villages, and all the people pulled on their strings and said:

"Come, Anansi. Come, Anansi."

"Come, Anansi. Come, Anansi."

"Come, Anansi. Come, Anansi."

"COME, ANANSI! COME, ANANSI!"

Anansi was pulled this way and that way, and his waist was mashed very, very thin. He didn't get any lunch at all because he had been so greedy. And to this day, Anansi the Spider still has a very narrow waist.

Anansi and Turtle

The Akan-speaking people call him Kwaku Ananse, the Tshi-speaking people call him Anansi. Here in the New World, in Jamaica, he is still called Annancy; in Haiti he is called Ti Malice. On the island of Curaçao he is called Nansi, and in some parts of the American South the name Anansi sounded like Aunt Nancy, so "he" became a "she!" This is another Anansi the Spider story from the Tshi-speaking people as told by Mary Furlough.

One day Anansi was just sitting down to the table in his house to eat some baked yams. Now, Turtle had been crawling all day, traveling from one place to another, and just as he came to Anansi's house he smelled the most delicious food he had ever smelled. Since he had been traveling all day he was hungry, so he went up to Anansi's house and knocked.

Anansi came to the doorway looking real mean, hoping that whoever had knocked would go away. He

pretended not to see Turtle, and gazed up high as he looked out the door.

"Down here," said Turtle, who is very low to the ground.

"Oh, it's you, Turtle," said Anansi. "What do you want?"

"Well, I have been traveling all day," said Turtle, "and I was wondering if you would share your meal with me."

Now, Anansi looked down at Turtle and said, "Oh, all right. Come on in here." For, you see, it was the polite custom in Anansi's country to share your meal with anyone who came to your door at mealtime. Anansi brought Turtle in and said, "Sit down. Have a seat." Turtle crawled up to the table and sat in a chair. "Help yourself," said Anansi.

Turtle was just about to help himself to the baked yams on the table when Anansi hollered out, "Turtle, don't you know better than to come to the table with dirty hands?" Turtle looked down at his hands, and sure enough, they were dirty because he'd been crawling all day. So Turtle got up and went outside to the creek. He washed his hands, and for good measure, he washed his face, too. By the time he got back to the house and crawled up on the chair, Anansi had already started to eat.

But as Turtle started to help himself, Anansi said again, "Turtle, I told you, you can't come to the table and help yourself with dirty hands." Turtle looked down and, sure enough, his hands were dusty again because he had crawled back up the trail from the creek, and the trail was dusty. So Turtle got down from his place and started down the trail again. In the meantime, Anansi was eating as fast as he could, stuffing his face, trying to eat everything so he wouldn't have to share.

Turtle got down to the creek and washed his hands again, but this time, when he came out of the creek he made sure he crawled back on the grass. He got back to the house, back up to his place at the table, and started to help himself. But Anansi was just stuffing the last bite of yams into his mouth!

Turtle looked at Anansi and said slowly, "Thank you for sharing your meal with me, Anansi. If you're ever in my part of the country, why don't you come by and share a meal with me?" Turtle crawled down and went on his way.

Anansi thought about it and thought about it, and wanted to enjoy that free meal at Turtle's house. Finally, after a few weeks, he couldn't stand it any longer, so he set out to find where Turtle lived. Anansi got up early one morning and began to travel. He crept from one bush to another, all day long, just taking his time, until he finally came to the place where Turtle lived. Now Turtle lived at the bottom of the creek, but as Anansi walked up, Turtle was sitting on the bank sunning himself. It was just about the supper hour!

Turtle looked at Anansi and said, "Welcome, Anansi. Did you come to share a meal with me?"

"Yes, yes," said Anansi.

"All right, Anansi," said Turtle. "You sit here on the bank and wait while I go set the table." Turtle dived down under the creek to his house. Anansi was up on the bank, dancing around on all his legs. He couldn't wait. Finally, Turtle came up and said, "Come down, Anansi. The table is all ready."

Turtle dived down under the water and sat at his table. Anansi jumped in the water to dive like Turtle did, but he went just under the surface of the water and then popped back up and floated on the top. He tried to dive again, and went just below the surface of the water, then popped back up and floated on the top. He stuck his head under the water and he could see Turtle down there, under the creek, slowly eating his meal. There was a plate set for Anansi, but he couldn't get to it. Anansi swam to the edge of the creek and climbed a tree. He jumped off, he dived off, he climbed up and did a belly-flop—but every time he hit the water he would go just under the surface a little bit and then pop right back up and float. Anansi just could not get himself to sink!

But Anansi was not about to miss his chance for a free meal. He swam to the shore and danced about on all his legs, trying to think of a way to get down to Turtle's table. "I know," he said out loud. "I've got pockets!" So he started picking up pebbles and putting them in his jacket pockets. Then he jumped back in the water, sank right down, and landed in the chair Turtle had set out for him.

There was the most beautiful banquet Anansi had ever seen on that table! Turtle had clams, he had eel, he had lily pads, he even had watercress sandwiches. He had everything Anansi could think of. And Turtle was sitting there, helping himself to that fine meal, very slowly.

Anansi filled his bowl with some of each delicious kind of food and was just about to start eating when Turtle looked at Anansi and said, "In my country, one must always take off his jacket before sitting at the table." It was true; Turtle had taken off his own jacket before sitting down to eat.

Anansi looked at the food, looked at Turtle, and slowly took off his jacket with the pebbles in the pockets. The jacket sank to the bottom and Anansi popped back up to the surface and floated on top. Below him, he could see Turtle slowly finishing his meal.

When you set out to outsmart someone, there's usually someone out there who can outsmart *you*.

Fling-A-Mile

In Jamaica, the African word Anansi, which is also sometimes said as Ananzi, is often spelled Annancy. The Jamaican stories are told in English, but they use many African ideas that create words we are not used to hearing. Retold from folklore, inspired by the stories of Miss Lou, this tale tells of Anansi's mixture of curiosity and greed. It reminds us of an ill-mannered child, and it always gets him in trouble. Fling-A-Mile is a mythical creature, not based on any real animal.

One day Anansi was walking along the riverbank looking for something to eat. He saw a strange hole in the mud of the riverbank, like the hole of a crawdad. Thinking there might be something to kill and eat inside, he reached in with one hand. Something grabbed hold of him!

"Who's got a-hold of me?" asked Anansi.

"Not me," said a voice down the hole.

"Not me who?" asked Anansi.

"Not me Fling-a-Mile," said the voice down the hole.

"I don't believe you can be a fling-a-mile," said Anansi. "Show me so that I can see."

The thing in the hole jerked Anansi off his feet and whirled him around and around and threw him a mile away along the riverbank. Anansi landed in the grass with a bounce, because Anansi is so lightweight. Anansi left a dent in the grass where he landed. He thought a minute and went back to the hole. He whistled as he crept up to the hole, like he hadn't been there before. Then he stuck his hand back down the hole. Something grabbed a-hold of him!

"Who's got a-hold of me?"

"Not me."

"Not me who?"

"Not me Fling-a-Mile."

"Fling me a mile so that I can see!"

The thing whirled Anansi around and around and threw him a mile down along the riverbank. Anansi landed in exactly the same spot as before, in the dent in the grass. Anansi went home and got a plate and a knife and a fork and a spoon. He cut a stake of wood and sharpened both ends really sharp. He went back to the riverbank, found the dent in the grass, and stuck the stake in, leaning toward the fling-a-mile hole. He put down the plate and the knife and the fork and the spoon and went to the riverbank to wait.

Along the bank came Hog.

"Hello, Hog."

"Hello, Anansi."

"Let's walk along the riverbank and catch some fish."

"Yes, we'll go," said Hog. They walked along, with Hog on the side of the bank with the fling-a-mile hole, and Anansi over to the other side. Soon Hog came to the hole.

"What a fine hole before you," said Anansi. "Reach in and see if there's anything to eat." Hog reached in and something grabbed a-hold of him.

"Something's got a-hold of me!"

"Ask him who's got a-hold of you."

"Who's got a-hold of me?" asked Hog.

"Not me."

"Ask him, 'Not me who?'" said Anansi.

"Not me who?"

"Not me Fling-a-Mile."

"Tell him you don't believe him. Make him show you so you can see," said Anansi.

"Show me so I can see," said Hog.

The thing lifted Hog off his feet and swung him around and around and threw him a mile down along the riverbank. Hog landed right on that stake, and it killed him dead. Anansi built a fire and ate roast hog. Monkey was high in the tree and saw it all happen.

The next day Anansi went down to the riverbank to wait.

Along the bank came Goat.

"Hello, Goat."

"Hello, Anansi."

"Let's walk along the riverbank and eat some greens."

"Yes, we'll go," said Goat. They walked along, with Goat on the side of the river with the fling-a-mile hole, and Anansi over to the other side. Soon Goat came to the hole.

"What a fine hole before you. Reach in and see if there's any rivergreens inside." Goat reached in.

"Something's got a-hold of me."

"Ask him, 'Who's got a-hold of me?'"

"Who's got a-hold of me?"

"Not me."

"Ask him, 'Not me who?'" said Anansi.

"Not me who?"

"Not me Fling-a-Mile."

"Tell him you don't believe him. Make him show you so you can see," said Anansi.

"Show me so I can see."

The thing lifted Goat off his feet and whirled him around and around and threw him a mile down along the riverbank. Goat landed right on that stake, and it killed him dead. Anansi built a fire and ate roast goat. Monkey was high in the tree and saw it all happen.

The next day Anansi went down to the riverbank to wait.

Along came Monkey, down from the tree without Anansi seeing him.

"Hello, Monkey."

"Hello, Anansi."

"Let's walk along the riverbank and eat some bananas."

"Yes, we'll go," said Monkey. They walked along, with Monkey on the side of the river with the fling-a-mile hole, and Anansi over to the other side. Soon Monkey came to the hole.

"What a fine hole before you. Reach in and see if any fruit fell in there."

"No, something might grab a-hold of me," said Monkey.

"Nothing's going to grab a-hold of you," said Anansi. "Reach in!"

"There's no fruit in that hole. You come reach in," said Monkey.

Anansi came over. "See, nothing's going to grab a-hold of you," said Anansi, putting his hand just barely into the hole.

Monkey grabbed Anansi's hand and shoved it far, far in. Anansi jumped and yelled, "Something's got a-hold of me!"

"Ask him who's got a-hold of you," said Monkey.

"Who's … got … a-hold of me?" said Anansi, pretending not to know.

"Not me."

"Ask him, 'Not me who?'" said Monkey, innocently.

"Not … me … who?" said Anansi, very weakly.

"Not me Fling-a-Mile."

"Tell him you don't believe him. Make him show you so you can see," said Monkey, cheerfully.

"Show … me … so … I … can … see," said Anansi in a whisper.

Fling-a-Mile lifted Anansi off his feet and wheeled him around and around.

"Oh, Monkey," said Anansi, wheeling around, "I got some cutlery down on the riverbank. Would you go and take it home for me and pull up my roasting stake, too?" begged Anansi, his voice getting louder as he was swung over Monkey's head.

Monkey said, "Yes, I'll go," and off he ran. But when he got to the wooden stake he just sat down and waited. Here came Anansi flying through the air.

"Mmmmmmmoooooonnnnkkkkeeeeyyyy!" he yelled as he fell.

Anansi landed on the stake, and it killed him dead. Monkey built a fire and roasted Anansi and had a fine dinner, for a monkey.

Jack Mandora, I don't choose any!*

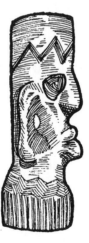

---

* By Heaven's Doors, I don't blame anyone in particular for such bad behavior!

Anansi and Candlefly

Anansi never seems to learn his lesson; his greed always gets the better of him. In this story retold from folklore, it's the giant firefly that is the victim of Anansi's greed.

Anansi's fire went out one day because he was careless. He knew his neighbor Candlefly, the huge firefly of Jamaica, would have a fine fire on his hearth. Anansi went to Candlefly's house and asked for some fire. Candlefly gave him some fire, and also, being a good neighbor, gave Anansi some eggs he had gathered. Anansi took the fire and the eggs and went home and had a good eat.

The next day, Anansi let his fire go out on purpose, and went over to Candlefly's. Candlefly gave him fire, and to be a good neighbor, gave him some more eggs. Anansi took the fire and the eggs and started for his house. Anansi was getting sweet-mouthed, or greedy, for those eggs, so he let the fire go out on the way home. He went back to Candlefly's house again. Candlefly gave him fire yet again. Anansi waited for

Candlefly to give him even more eggs. He waited and waited. Candlefly never gave him one more.

Even though Anansi still had the eggs from that day in his pouch, called a side bag, he lied to Candlefly and said, "Brother Candlefly, when the fire burned out, it burned my hand. Will you give me one more egg to wet my hand and make it feel better?"

Candlefly gave him one more egg.

"If you will come late tonight, Brother Anansi," said Candlefly, "I will take you to where I gather eggs and you can gather all the eggs you like."

Anansi went home. He didn't wait until night to go back. He barely waited until afternoon, he was so sweet-mouthed for the eggs. He went out every few minutes to look at the sun. He was at Candlefly's before the sun was down. He had a long bag with him.

Candlefly led Anansi out in the trees to look for bird eggs. Each time Candlefly would open his wings, his bright light would shine out from the gash between the wings. Each time they saw an egg in Candlefly's light, Anansi would grab it.

"Me, I saw it first," Anansi would say each time.

Each time Candlefly flashed his light, Anansi took the egg. Candlefly didn't get a single egg. Anansi was so rude he took them all.

Candlefly said, "Good night, Anansi," and he quickly flew off home. Anansi was in the dark. He had no light of his own.

Anansi began to grope his way in the darkness. The night was cloudy and Anansi couldn't see anything. He stumbled along the path until he bucked onto a house, bumped right into it.

He couldn't see the house and he didn't know whose house it was, but he began to scheme, and called out, "Godfather?"

"Who's that calls?" said a deep voice inside the house.

"Anansi, your godson. I brought some eggs for you!"

Tiger was inside his house, and he didn't have a godson. But he did know Anansi, and hated him for tricks he had pulled in the past. Tiger opened the door.

Anansi swallowed hard at the sight of Tiger.

"Godfather Tiger, good morning," he said.

"Come in, Godson," said Tiger. And he shut the door tight behind Anansi. Tiger told his wife to put the big copper kettle on the fire. They boiled the whole barrel bag of eggs. When the eggs were ready, Tiger and his wife and children sat and ate the eggs.

"Do you want any eggs, Godson?" said Tiger with a sharp-toothed grin.

Anansi was afraid. "No, thanks," he said.

While Anansi sat and watched the fire, Tiger went and put a lobster from a bucket into the bowl where the eggs had been. He put some eggshells in so it looked like there were eggs left. Then he noisily put the bowl down near Anansi.

"Stay for the night, Godson," said Tiger with his sharp-toothed grin. He licked the eggs from his lips.

Anansi swallowed hard.

Tiger knew how much Anansi loved eggs. Anansi saw the shells and thought there were whole boiled eggs still in the bowl. When everyone was asleep, the lamp burned out. Anansi reached for the egg bowl.

Lobster's claw gave Anansi a good pinch. Anansi jumped.

"What's the matter, Godson?" asked Tiger in the dark.

"A dog-flea bit me," said Anansi. "I never before saw a dog-flea as big as you have in your yard, on your property here."

A few minutes later, Anansi yelled again.

"You've got the biggest dog-fleas!" he said.

He tried and tried all night, but he never got an egg. Just lobster pinches.

The next morning, Tiger stretched out hard and said, "I'm sorry you got so bit by dog-fleas last night, Godson. You're the first one ever came to my yard who said dog-fleas bit him."

"I didn't sleep at all from the time I went to bed until now," said Anansi.

Tiger's wife fixed the morning tea. That meant it was time for the guest to leave. Anansi drank the tea with Tiger and his wife. Then Tiger said, "Go to my goat pen, Godson, and bring me the goat that you find there," since the host usually asked a favor of an overnight guest.

Tiger was out of the house when Anansi went out to the goat pen. Sure enough, there was a goat, a big old goat with a long, long beard. Anansi took a stick and beat the goat. "Your master ate all the eggs, and I didn't get any one, not even one." he yelled.

The goat spoke, "You're ungrateful, Godson. You'd make a good lunch." The goat pulled off his beard and it was Tiger with a goat hide over him. Anansi let out a scream as Tiger started toward him.

Anansi screamed again and ran as Tiger took after him. Anansi ran back past the house and saw a water gourd. He ran and hid inside it. Tiger came around the corner and couldn't see Anansi anywhere. He growled angrily.

Tiger's wife came out and took up the gourd. She put it on her head and started to go get water. Anansi was inside. He knew that Tiger's wife was very dutiful.

"Your man is all sick from eating so many eggs," he whispered.

Tiger's wife looked around to see who spoke.

A minute later, Anansi spoke again, "Your man is all sick from eating so many eggs."

Tiger's wife stopped on the trail and listened and looked, but she couldn't see who spoke. She started on again.

A minute later, Anansi spoke again, "Your man is all sick from eating so many eggs."

Tiger's wife threw the gourd down and ran back to the house. Tiger was fine.

Anansi came out of the gourd and ran for home.

Every time after that, if Anansi went to Candlefly's house, Candlefly's wife would say, "He's gone a long time. Come back next month."

Anansi never went egg hunting with Candlefly again. And he never found that place where Candlefly found so many bird eggs, either.

Jack Mandora, I don't choose any!*

---

* I don't accuse any of my listeners of such bad behavior!

That Mule Won't Work

African-American hillfolks in Arkansas and Missouri were farmers who preserved some of their African trickster stories in the local folklore. The spider charac- ter has disappeared from the two following stories from Missouri, but both are well-known in Africa and Jamaica. There are dozens of African stories among the stories from Europe and from the native Americans that are still told in the Ozarks. This one is retold from Ozark folklore.

An old man and his young grandson lived all alone out on a farm by themselves. The boy was a good grandson, but some days he made excuses for not doing his work.

One day the grandfather said, "Go on down to that barn and hitch up that old mule, and go plow the north forty acres of our land."

The boy kind of dragged down to the barn and saw the mule standing there with his head down in the hay.

The boy thought the mule was eating the hay, but instead the mule was watching the boy.

The grandson came over to the mule, carrying the harness, and said, "Okay, Mule, let's go. Grandpa says to plow the north forty."

The old mule jerked his head up and looked the grandson straight in the eyes. "You go and tell your grandpa," said the mule, "that I ain't going to work today!"

Now, the grandson let out a holler and dropped the harness and ran back to the cabin where the grandfather was sitting on the porch.

"Grandpa! Grandpa!" said the boy. "That mule told me he ain't going to work today!"

The grandfather thought the boy was trying to get out of plowing the field, so he said, "You go back down there and tell that mule that he *is* going to work today."

Well, the grandson kind of bit his lip, and swallowed hard a couple of times, and turned and walked back to the barn. The old mule was watching the boy real close-like. The boy got to the barn, picked up the harness, and said, "Mule, Grandpa said you *is* going to work today."

The mule threw his head back, stamped the ground with one hoof, and said, "You go and tell your grandpa that I said I *ain't* going to work today!"

The boy ran back to the cabin and said, "Grandpa! That mule says to tell you that he *ain't* going to work today!"

Well, the grandfather decided that the boy just didn't want to do the work, so he said, "I'll go tell that blamed mule myself!" So he took his walking cane and smacked his lips to call his little black-and-white dog, and the three went off across the yard to the barn— man, boy, and dog.

The old man walked up to the mule. The mule had his head down like he was eating, but he wasn't really. The grandfather rapped the mule on the shin to get his attention and said out, "Now, Mule, I say you're going to plow!"

The mule reared his head up and snorted at the old man and said, "And I say I *ain't* going to plow!"

The old man let out a yell, and he and the boy and the dog ran all the way back past the cabin to the chopping stump before they stopped and sat down.

"I never heard of such a thing as a talking mule!" said the grandfather.

"Me neither," said the boy.

"I wouldn't have believed it if I hadn't seen it myself," said the little dog.

"Who ever heard of a talking mule!" said the ax.

"Not me," said the woodpile.

"I don't believe any of you," said the stump.

Clever Mollie

When this story, retold from Ozark folklore, was told in Africa, Mollie May was the servant of Anansi instead of that of a rich man. This story probably came at the same time to Jamaica and the mainland of the American South, for it is still told in both places today.

A rich man had a hill girl working for him as his maid. Her name was Mollie, and she was smart! But sometimes she was a little lazy. One day the rich man asked a rich friend to dinner and he told Mollie to cook the best. She cooked up two fine chickens, one for each man, and the rich man bought a bottle of fine wine. But the rich man wanted to put on airs for this other rich man. He said, "If only we had some of those finger sandwiches."

Mollie'd never heard of such a thing, but she said nothing.

The rich man went to fetch his friend, and Mollie set out the plates and poured two glasses of wine. She took a taste from the bottle to make sure it hadn't turned bad with age. It was good! She tasted it several times.

She also had to taste the chicken, to see if it came out all right. It was good. She tasted it several times, too. Pretty soon the wine was all gone from the bottle and the chicken was just bones.

Here came the rich man, putting on airs, bringing his friend along. He sat the friend in the dining room, in front of the plates and the glasses of wine. "If only we had finger sandwiches," he said again.

Mollie knew she'd have to think fast. When the rich man went to the sideboard to get the fancy carving knife for the chicken, Mollie came in and whispered to the guest. "He's gone crazy!" she said. "He's going to cut off your fingers and make finger sandwiches!"

Here came the rich man with the sharp knife. He was going to give it to the rich friend, so the friend could have the honor of carving the chickens. "Hold out your hand," he said.

The guest screamed and ran out the door.

"He took both your chickens," Mollie said to the rich man. "Go get 'em back from him!"

The rich man ran out with his carving knife, yelling to his friend, "Just let me have one! Just let me have one!"

The guest put his hands into his pockets and ran as fast as he could, and never saw the rich man again!

Mollie laughed and laughed, and the rich man never knew.

Clever Mollie!

Why Brother Alligator Has a Rough Back

Retold from Southern folklore and inspired by the stories of Mary Furlough, this story is from the Mbundu-speaking people of Angola.

Brother Alligator was lying beside the river, sunning himself. He was snoring and his mouth was half-open. His smooth, green back was as beautiful as Brother Cornsnake's.

Brother Rabbit came hopping along through the tall grass near the river, and he hopped right over Brother Alligator before he saw him. When he saw Brother 'Gator, he stopped and panted and panted. Just then, Brother Dog went crashing by in the grass, barking. Brother Alligator awoke and looked at Brother Rabbit.

"Brother Rabbit," said the 'gator, "why do you puff and blow so?"

"Brother Man sent Brother Dog to run me," said Brother Rabbit. "I think he had in mind to eat me for his supper. Uh … I hope *you* ain't hungry, Brother 'Gator."

Brother 'Gator just laughed a low, rumbling laugh. "I ate today," he said.

"Whew," said Brother Rabbit, relaxing now that he knew the 'gator wouldn't eat him. "I've got enough trouble for one day."

Brother 'Gator just laughed again, and stretched his smooth back and flipped his tail.

"You're laughing at me, Brother 'Gator!" said Brother Rabbit. "That ain't polite. You'll get your share of trouble some day."

Now, Brother 'Gator was laughing so hard that he scared away some flamingos from the river. "Trouble?" boomed Brother 'Gator. "Trouble? Nothing ever troubles me!"

"Nothing?" asked Brother Rabbit.

Brother Alligator swung his huge head around and looked at the rabbit with his dull eyes. His jagged teeth shone in the sun as he opened his gigantic mouth. Brother Rabbit shrank back, and the 'gator said, "Nothing!" After a moment he added. "I'd like to see somebody try to give me trouble!"

Now, Brother Rabbit was already planning. "Would you really?" he asked.

"Yessssss!" said Brother Gator. "I would."

"Well," said Brother Rabbit, swallowing hard, "I heard that Brother Trouble would be passing right by the river, here in the broom grass, tomorrow afternoon. I reckon that if you wanted to meet him, you could do it then!"

Brother 'Gator laughed again and said he'd be here, in the same place, if Trouble wanted to see him as bad as he wanted to see some trouble. Then he crawled to the bank and slid into the water.

The next day, Brother Rabbit came hopping by the broom grass and greeted Brother 'Gator. "Morning, Brother 'Gator," he said. "The dew has all gone and it's a fine day."

The old 'gator just gave a grunt and grinned his ragged grin.

"Brother Trouble is right over there in the broom grass. I saw him as I came by," said the rabbit. "C'mon over and meet him!" He hopped away.

Brother Alligator just turned and crawled slowly through the broom grass after the rabbit. When the old smooth-backed critter was far from the river, deep in the broom grass, he smelled something. Brother Rabbit had sat down at the edge of the grass and taken his pipe out of his vest pocket and lit it. Then he puffed for a moment and touched the pipe coals to the broom grass. Pretty soon the whole patch of grass was burning.

Brother Alligator turned ever-which way, lashing his big tail and looking for a way to escape. The fire burned him and burned him. He commenced to holler out, "Trouble! Trouble! Trouble!"

"Did Brother Trouble find you, Brother Alligator?" called out Brother Rabbit.

The 'gator thrashed his way through the broom grass and down to the riverbank. He crashed into the water to put out the fire. As he floated in the water, the grass fire burned itself out at the water's edge. He floated in the river, growling and grumbling. Off in the woods he could hear Brother Rabbit laughing. The smoke and steam drifted off Brother 'Gator's back. His back, which had been smooth, was now all rough and bumpy.

And it's been that way ever since.

You shouldn't trouble Trouble until Trouble troubles you.

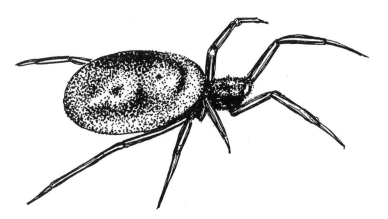

Parables About People

Many of the language groups of Africa live in the highlands, away from the rivers, and their stories focus on a different kind of adventure. The people in the river valleys tell mostly amusing fables about animals that poke fun at people's behavior. In the highlands, many of the stories are about people and how they face danger and fear.

In these stories, there is also a teaching message. The people in these stories provide examples of how to behave, or how not to behave. This kind of story, from which we learn wisdom, is called a parable.

When the animal fables were brought to America, they were "transplanted" and told as if they had happened here. These parables about people are directly from Africa, where they are still told. They came to America more recently, as more African people came to America after World War II. These parables are always told in such a way that the listener knows they are taking place in Africa, in the highlands.

The Faithful Brother

This is a story of the Kikuyu-speaking people of Kenya, retold from African folklore.

A long time ago there was a young warrior who lived with his sister. They lived alone on a homestead, far from any neighbors. Their parents had been killed by a wild animal when the warrior and his sister were young, and the two had taken care of each other as they grew up.

Because this was long ago, the warrior wore a goatskin hat that people no longer wear today. He wore his hair very long in back, but his sister shaved the front for him.

The warrior often went away for days at a time on long hunting trips. Each time when he came home, his sister had hot gruel waiting, and they sat on stools and talked. They loved each other very much.

One day the warrior had been gone for two days and the sister was making gruel for them both, hoping that he would return soon. A strange man came to the door of the hut. The strange man could see from the way the girl dressed and wore her hair that she was not married. He took her by the wrist and stole her to be his bride. This was a custom in those days.

When the warrior came home, he called to his sister. She was not in the house, but he heard her calling back to him from far away in the tall grass.

"Go into the hut, Brother," she called, "and eat your gruel. It is waiting on your stool."

The warrior did not go into the hut. He followed the trail left in the tall grass by the strange man who was stealing his sister. He was a good tracker, but the man and the sister were moving fast. Gradually they got further and further away from the warrior, but he never gave up the search.

As he followed the trail, the young warrior became hungry, but he dared not stop to hunt. Instead, he began to chew on the goatskin hat. As days turned into weeks he ate all his hat, along with some roots and fruits he gathered. He became very dirty and tired searching for his sister. He ate very little and became thin. He had no one to shave the hair above his forehead and the hair grew long.

He came to a homestead, a very long journey from his own. He was tired and hungry and many months had passed. There he was met at the doorway by a married woman who looked frightened. He asked for food and she gave him some in a broken bowl. He took the food and ate outside. He slept the night on the ground outside the hut, so as not to worry her.

The next morning the woman came out and he greeted her. They walked together to the field and he helped her scare the birds away from the crops, because the grain was ripe.

As he scared the birds, he sang:

> Fly away, little birds,
> Fly away, little birds.
> Like my sister has flown away.
> I have never seen her again.

The woman looked at him in surprise and said, "Why has your sister flown away from you?"

The warrior answered, "I do not know. She left me many months ago and I have followed her footprints and those of a man for a long, long ways."

The woman's eyes grew large. "She did not tell you where she was going?" asked the woman.

"All she said," the warrior answered, "was, 'Your gruel is on the stool.'"

The woman began to weep.

"I am your sister," she said. "Your hair is grown out and you are thin and dirty from the trail. I did not know you."

When her husband came home, the dutiful sister had fed and clothed her loyal brother, shaved his forehead, and put on him the armbands of a warrior. The husband welcomed the brother and in time they all became one family. The husband paid the warrior a good and fair price for his bride, the warrior's sister. In time the warrior went out and bought himself a bride as well. The two families had their homesteads side by side, and the brother and sister lived as neighbors all the days of their lives.

Meat of the Tongue

This story, as told by Lloyd Wilson, is a parable of the Swahili-speaking people of Africa about the relationship between men and women.

Many years ago, in a land far away, a great sultan lived in a palace with his wife. But the queen was very bored and unhappy. She would wander through the palace, moping, yawning, and crying to herself, "What am I going to do? I am so bored and frustrated."

The queen began to lose weight, and her hair began to fall out. Her skin was all pimply and her eyes were bloodshot red. She was, indeed, an unhappy queen.

Now, in the village there lived a poor man whose wife was always very happy. When she worked in her garden, she would sing songs to herself and call out to her neighbors, "Hello, isn't it a beautiful day? Hope you're feeling well." The poor man's wife was a healthy, lovable, kind, and friendly woman. Her skin was nice and taut, and soft like a baby's.

Well, the sultan heard about the poor man's wife and immediately summoned him to the palace.

"Poor man," said the sultan, "why is it that your wife is always so happy and beautiful and my queen is sad and frustrated? Tell me, poor man, what is your secret?"

"My Sultan," said the poor man, "I have no secret. I merely feed my wife meat of the tongue."

"Meat of the tongue?" whispered the sultan thoughtfully. All around, the advisors also whispered amongst themselves, "Meat of the tongue?" So, the sultan summoned the butcher and told him he must sell to him, the sultan, exclusively, all the tongues of every beast in his shop. The butcher smiled and went away. The next day, he sent all the tongues of every beast in his shop to the palace. And these, the royal cook had to prepare in all manner of elegant dishes. There was tongue stew, tongue soup, fillet of tongue, tongue fricassee, barbecued tongue, and roast tongue. There was tongue pie and tongue casserole, tongue salad, and tongue under glass. And this the queen had to eat, sometimes three and four times a day. But she would not gain weight, she remained bored and frustrated, and no matter what the sultan did he could not make his queen happy.

The sultan became angry and summoned the poor man once again. "Poor man, you have deceived me! For this you must exchange wives."

So, the poor man reluctantly gave up his own wife and took the lean queen home.

As time passed, it became clear that the new queen would not thrive in the palace. She began to grieve and weep. The fine jewels and gold did not interest her. She no longer would sing out hellos, she lost weight, and no matter how hard the sultan tried, he could not satisfy his new queen. Everyone could see that the new queen was very unhappy.

But, alas, when the poor man came home, he would tell his wife of all the things he had seen and done during the day, especially the funny things. The poor man would play his kalimba, his thumb piano, and they would sing songs and laugh and talk until way in the middle of the night. The poor man's new wife began to smile. She no longer lost her hair nor weight. Her skin was now taut and soft like that of a baby, and she smiled to herself as she worked in her garden, remembering all of the wonderful things her new husband had told her the night before. The queen had become very happy.

Now, there came a time when the sultan grew tired of his new wife and summoned his old wife to return to the palace. But she refused! This so infuriated the sultan that he went in person to bring his wife back to the palace. But when he saw how beautiful she had become, and how happy she was, the sultan asked, "Wife of mine, what has this poor man done to you?"

And she told him. And it was then he understood "meat of the tongue."

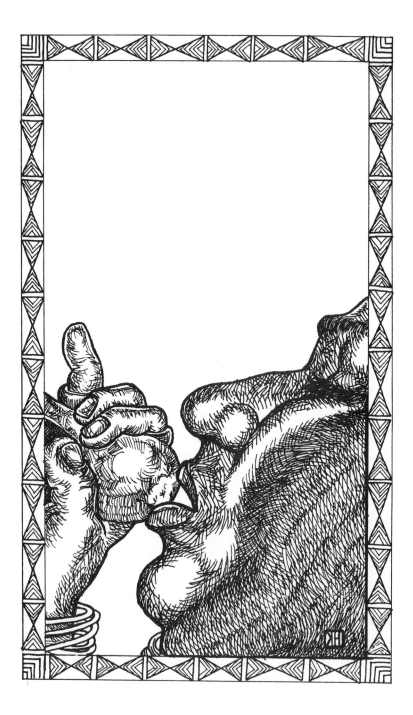

The Gluttonous Rich Man

This is a story of the Karamba-speaking people, retold from African folklore.

Once there was a rich man who was very fat. He had inherited land and cattle from his father and he grew fat because he did not need to work. As he ate more, he loved eating more. He forgot to thank his servants for their work, and he never complimented his wife's good cooking anymore. He was just too busy eating. He began to think that he couldn't ever get enough to eat. Then he began to think that his wife and servants weren't trying their best to please him with the food they prepared.

Soon he complained at every meal.

His good wife got so tired of hearing him complain that she went to her father's village for a long visit and left the servants to do the cooking. While she was gone the servants got so tired of hearing him complain that they all quit their jobs and went to work for kinder people in other parts of the village.

The rich man tried cooking for himself. At least now he didn't worry that someone was eating the best part of the meal and leaving the scraps to serve to him. So he ate even more.

When he found out he didn't like butchering and cooking for himself, he decided to go to his father-in-law's village and ask his wife to come home. When he arrived, his father-in-law gave him a goat as a gift, which was a custom in that village.

The rich man butchered the goat, cooked it on a fire in the compound yard, and ate it. He hadn't eaten for many hours and a goat was just a snack to him now. He was still hungry, he thought, and he saw a sheep on the other side of a fencerow. He thought it was his father-in-law's sheep, so he killed it and was about to butcher it.

His wife came out of her father's house and cried out, "That is not our sheep! That is the sheep of the chief, whose compound lies next to ours!"

Since her husband was a stranger and a bit of a fool, she decided to cover his error for him. They took the sheep and laid it beside the chief's horse, which was tied to a tree near the fencerow. It looked as if the horse had killed the sheep. The woman then went to the chief's house and said, "One of your sheep is lying beside your horse." She had not told a lie. The chief looked out and saw the sheep beside the horse, who was pawing the ground, smelling the blood of the sheep. The chief thought the horse had killed the sheep.

The next day the rich man was hungry again, and his wife took a basket and went to the cornfield. She gathered enough corn to feed ten men. When the corn was roasted and her husband and family had eaten, the corn was gone. The rich man left the house, took up the basket by the front door, and went to the fields. There he wandered about, picking corn from anywhere he felt like, even though most of the corn he picked belonged to other people.

When he got back to the compound, his wife saw all the corn and cried out, "That is not our corn! I see corn from many different people's fields in that basket!"

Since her husband was a stranger in this village and actually quite a fool, she decided to cover his error for him. She put the basket of corn at the edge of the fields and then let some cows out of their enclosure by taking down a few fence poles. The cows went into the fields and began to knock down the corn plants and eat the corn. Then she went to her neighbors' houses and called to them.

"The cows are out in the corn. I have picked up much of what I found, but I need help!" she said. She had not told a lie.

All the neighbors ran out and herded the cows back to their enclosure, and picked up the rest of the corn the cows had knocked down. Then they quickly sorted the corn and everyone went home with their own corn. Everyone thought the cows were to blame.

The next day the woman ground millet in a grinding bowl and made milletmeal. She mixed the meal with water and other things and cooked millet cakes from the meal. After everyone had eaten, and the foolish husband had eaten enough for five people, the husband was still hungry. When no one was around, he took the grinding bowl and began to lick the unused meal out of it. He was still hungry! Soon his face was so far down into the deep, heavy grinding bowl that he got his head stuck in it. He called for help.

The woman's family gathered and tried not to laugh at the man with his head stuck in a bowl. Because he was a stranger in the village and was so spoiled that he didn't know much about cooking or grinding, his wife decided to cover his error for him.

"It is all my fault," she said. "I said he had a thick head. He said he didn't. I said his head was so thick it wouldn't even go into the grinding bowl. He said it would."

Everyone laughed and helped the rich man get his head unstuck. He was so embarrassed he said goodbye and went back home to his own village. At home, he sent his one remaining servant back to tell his wife to come home. The servant returned that night.

"Where is my wife?" asked the gluttonous rich man. "What did she say?"

The servant tried not to smile as he told the rich man, "Your wife said that if you think she's ever coming back here, your head is even thicker than she thought."

The gluttonous rich man had to cook for himself after that, and he became very slim in a few years.

Three Young Men Who Go Out to Find Death

This is the way storyteller Sarah McCoy tells this story. She learned it in 1982 from a storyteller with the Ashanti Family Players. It is the origin of Geoffrey Chaucer's "Pardoner's Tale" in his Canterbury Tales. *Chaucer cited his original source as 'coming from some part of Africa.'*

There once lived three young men who were brothers. They were angry young men, angry because death had taken their mother and father. Death had also taken other friends and relatives.

The three brothers were talking one day, when the oldest looked at the younger two and said, "Do you know what we should do? We should go out and find death, and kill death. If we find death, and kill death, then no one else will ever die."

Now, when the oldest said this to the younger two, they thought this was a good idea. They all packed their bags and started out on a journey to find death and kill death.

Now, in those days it was very common for travelers to meet other travelers along the way, and for one to want to know where another was going or what another was about. So, someone would see the young men and ask, "Where are you going?"

And they would answer, "We are going out to find death and kill death."

Now, some, on hearing this answer, thought it was strange; some laughed, thinking it was funny. But everyone who asked was given the same answer.

One day as the young men were traveling, they saw an old man sitting on the side of the road. This old man, like all the others, wanted to know where the three young men were going, so he asked.

The oldest of the three looked at the old man and said, "We are going out to find death and kill death."

The old man looked at the three young men and said, "Go home. Live your lives and be happy and forget this thing."

The oldest brother looked at the old man and said, "Can't you see that death has taken our mother and our father? Can't you see he takes our relatives and friends? If we find death and kill death, no one else will ever die."

The old man looked at the three young men and said, "It seems to me as if I can say nothing to change your mind. And since I cannot change your mind, let me make the job easy for you. I will tell you where to find death."

When the old man said this, the three brothers listened.

"You should go down this road five miles," the old man said. "You will come to a fork in the road. Stay to the right and walk another two miles, and you will come to a great tree. Dig underneath the tree and you will find death."

The young men thanked the old man and hurried down the road. They went five miles and came to the fork in the road. They went to the right and walked two miles, and came to the great tree. The young men began to dig under the tree and what they found was a wooden box. They opened up the box and looked inside. What they found inside was seven gold coins.

The three young men forgot about finding death and killing death, and started talking about how they could divide the coins.

The oldest said, "Well, there are three of us and there are seven coins. We could each take two coins and then draw straws. The one with the short straw could take the extra coin and go to town and buy bread and wine. We could eat bread and drink wine, and we would each still have two coins."

They drew straws and the youngest drew the short straw. He took the extra coin and started to town to buy the bread and wine, but as he walked to town he thought, "I could buy bread and wine and I could also buy poison, and poison the wine. My brothers will drink and I will not. They will die and I will have six coins."

The oldest and middle brothers waited at the great tree. The oldest looked at the middle brother and said,

"Do you know what we should do? We should hide in the brush and wait for our youngest brother to return. We should kill him, and we will each have three coins."

The youngest brother went into town and bought the bread and wine. He also bought poison and poisoned the wine. He started back to the great tree.

Just as the youngest approached the great tree, the oldest and middle brothers jumped out of the brush and killed him. After they killed him, they decided to sit down and eat the bread and drink the wine.

And then they all found death.

Bigger Than Life

In addition to animal fables and parables about people, which came first from Africa, there is another popular style of story told today. These stories all originated here in America, telling about the lives of African Americans whose adventures seemed bigger than real life normally allows.

Often the truth about these men and women was lost in the exciting fantasy that storytellers added down through the years, as the stories passed from generation to generation. When there was more fun and fantasy to the story than to the truth, these once-true tales turned into partly-true legends.

The characters in these legends lived between 1800 and 1900, long enough ago that the stories about their lives have become bigger than life.

John Henry

John Henry was a real live man, and the basis of this story is almost certainly the truth—but it is such a good story that many different states in the U.S.A. claim John Henry as their native son. Here is his story, retold from folklore and inspired by the stories of Tyrone Wilkerson.

Working on the American railroads laying track was hard, hard work. But the pay was good, and the men took pride in what they did, laying the shining rails that would connect all parts of the nation. And the finest man ever to lay track was John Henry!

Some folks say John Henry was born in Mississippi, others say Tennessee, but wherever he came from, he was a mighty, mighty man. He layed track for the Chesapeake and Ohio Railroad. When the heavy wooden ties were laid on the prepared railbed, iron rails were set in place on top of them. Then men with twelve-pound, long-handled hammers drove iron spikes to hold the rails on the ties, the way a nail holds two boards together. The men worked in fours to drive the spikes. They stood in a circle, each hitting the spike once, then raising his huge hammer while the other three hit the spike once each. When the men got going, the hammers hit four times in a second and rang like church bells.

When the hammers were ringing, the men sometimes sang in rhythm with them. John Henry had the most beautiful bass voice, and the men often asked him to sing as they worked. Ladies from whatever town they were near would come out to the railbed just to hear John Henry sing. But John Henry didn't do more than smile at the pretty ladies, because he had the prettiest wife in the countryside. Her name was Polly, and John Henry always called her Pretty Polly.

Pretty Polly could cook the sweetest sweet potato pie, and then go down to the railbed, pick up a hammer, and drive spikes in her husband's place when he got sick. This only happened once, in 1872, but it was still really something.

When the C&O Railroad got to the mountains of West Virginia, the men had to dig a tunnel through the rock of the mountain. To break the solid rock they used big drills, powered by a steam engine, that made a deep hole in the stone. Then they put dynamite in the hole and blasted the rock away. Finally, the men used their hammers and drove big iron spikes three feet long into the rock, to break it away and open up a tunnel. The work was hard and slow.

One day the boss of the track-laying crew brought in a special steam-powered drill that could drive spikes with a heavy metal arm. It worked like a man with a hammer. The boss told the men the railroad company wasn't happy with how long the work was taking, and had sent this steam drill, which ran on the rails as it laid them.

The men of the track-laying crew were angry that the railroad officials had brought in a steam hammer. If the steam hammer worked faster than *they* could, they might all lose their jobs. Most of the men had families, and needed this work badly. They all turned to John Henry. If anyone could save them, *he* could!

John Henry picked up his hammer and walked slowly over to the track where two rails lay in place waiting to be fastened with spikes. John Henry stood and watched as the steam hammer was slowly rolled along the rails and up to the first undriven spike. John Henry took the right side of the track, and the steam hammer was set in place along the left side of the track. The boss threw the lever that started the steam hammer, and John Henry swung his hammer high in the air and brought it down on a spike.

The steam hammer huffed and puffed and the metal arm rose and fell with a dull thud, so fast it sounded like the rumble of distant thunder. John Henry swung his hammer faster and faster till sparks shot off the iron spikes like lightning, and the steel hammer rang out like giant silver bells. John Henry's sweaty body glowed like he was made of gold in the light of the lanterns in the tunnel. Ten spikes had been driven, five by the steam hammer and five by John Henry. Then a hundred had been driven, forty-six by the steam hammer and fifty-four by John Henry. Then two hundred spikes had been driven, ninety-one by the steam hammer and one hundred and nine by John Henry. Slowly John Henry pulled ahead. When the steam hammer had laid nine feet of track and John Henry had laid fourteen feet, the boss shut the steam engine off.

John Henry had won.

But he had worked so hard that his great heart burst from the strain and he died with his hammer in his hand. He was buried in the tunnel, right where he died, and when the trains go by his grave, they always blow their whistles in a long, low, sad call that sounds like the words, "There ... lies a steel-drivin' man."

"John Henry"—The Song

Resung from folklore and inspired by the songs of Tyrone Wilkerson.

John Henry, he could hammer,
  He could whistle, he could sing.
  He would whistle up every morning
  Just to hear his hammer ring.

When John Henry was a little baby,
Sittin' on his daddy's knee,
He picked up a hammer and a little piece of steel;
Said, "This hammer'll be the death of me,
Lord, Lord, hammer be the death of me!"

When John Henry's family needed money,
Said he didn't have but a dime.
"If you wait until the red sun goes down,

I'll get it from the man in the mine,
Lord, Lord, I'll get it from the man in the mine."

Well, John Henry went to the Captain.
The Captain said, "What can you do?"
"I can heist a jack, I can lay your track,
I can pick and shovel, too.
Lord, Lord, I can pick and shovel, too!"

The Captain said to John Henry,
"I'm goin' t'bring me a steam drill 'round.
I'm goin' t'bring a steam drill out of the town.
I'm goin' t'hub that steel on down,
Lord, Lord, hub that steel on down."

John Henry said to the Captain,
"A man ain't nothin' but a man,
Before I let your steam drill beat me down
I'll die with my hammer in my hand,
Lord, Lord, die with my hammer in my hand."

Well, John Henry drove into the mountain.
His hammer was strikin' fire.
He drove so hard, his poor heart broke.
He laid down his hammer and he died,
Lord, Lord, laid down his hammer and he died.

Then John Henry went on up to Heaven.
And they buried him in the sand.
And ev'ry lonesome stranger that passes by him
     says,
"There lies a steel-drivin' man,

Lord, Lord, there lies a steel-drivin' man.
There lies a steel-drivin' man!
Lord! Lord! There lies a steel-drivin' man!"

Annie Christmas

*Like John Henry, Annie Christmas was most probably
a real person, and she is so popular in folklore that many
different kinds of people claim her as their heroine. The
story has grown, though, with years of retelling. Here
it is retold from folklore and inspired by the stories of
Jackie Torrence.*

The life of a keelboat pilot on the lower Mississippi
River was a dangerous life in the late 1800s. Rough
characters lived and worked on the river and no sissy
or weakling ever lasted very long out on the dark,
rolling waters. A lot of tough men worked the river—
and one tough woman.

She was born on Christmas Day, and folks called
her Annie Christmas. Annie Christmas was six-foot-
six-inches tall in her stocking feet and she weighed 250
pounds. She could carry a barrel of flour under each
arm as she loaded her keelboat—and balance a third
barrel on her head! When her boat was loaded, she

would pilot it to some other town along the river and sell the merchandise to make a profit.

She stayed on her keelboat almost all the time, but when the water was rising and the towns were in danger of being flooded, she would put on pants and go work on the levees with the men, stacking bags of sand to hold the river within its banks. She saved many lives and made many friends on the Mississippi.

Most of all, people loved Annie Christmas because she was strong, and honest, and hated bullies. If some big fellow was picking on someone helpless, out of nowhere came Annie Christmas. Sometimes the bullies would take her on and fight Annie. But not very often, because whenever she fought with a bully, she won! And she ordered them off the river and made them go somewhere else to live and work.

After years of beating the bullies on the river, Annie had a necklace made of all the noses she'd bitten off, and ears she'd torn off, and eyeballs she'd snatched out of bullies' heads. She was one tough woman!

Annie Christmas fell in love with a gambler named Riverboat Charlie. He was the handsomest man on the river and Annie loved his laugh and his looks and his luck. Charlie loved Annie for her bravery and her brashness and her brawn. They had twelve fine sons, who were all born on the same day and all grew to be seven feet tall. They were the crew on Annie's keelboat, and Charlie rode the river on steamboats, gambling to pay for all the food the boys ate.

One time Charlie played the roulette wheel for twenty-four hours without resting and he was winning almost every spin of the wheel. Then, as the sun was coming up after a long night, he leaned over the wheel and bet on red. Each time the wheel was spun the little ball landed in a red pocket and Charlie won. People watching him play thought that sooner or later he would change the color he bet on to black, but he just kept looking down at the wheel and left all his money bet on red. Time and again the wheel was spun, and each time the marble landed on red. Each time Charlie's winnings got bigger. Finally, the owner of the riverboat came out to Charlie and told him he couldn't bet any more, he'd won all the money in the boat's bank. When the man touched Charlie's shoulder to congratulate him, Charlie fell over.

Riverboat Charlie was dead!

Charlie had died of exhaustion hours before, but because he was hunched over, and so incredibly calm when he gambled, no one had realized he was dead. All the money he won was given to Annie and the boys.

But Annie's heart was broken by Charlie's death, and she, too, died not long afterwards. The twelve boys put Annie's body in a black coffin on a black barge and let it float slowly down the Mississippi and out into the Gulf of Mexico, where it disappeared under the dark waves. Then they piloted Annie's keelboat up the Mississippi and took jobs in the big cities of the North because they couldn't stand to work the river now that Annie was gone.

Casey Jones and His Friends

Just about the most famous popular song of the first half of the twentieth century was "Casey Jones." Now, Casey Jones was a white man, but his two friends Simpson Webb and Wallace Saunders were black, and they are the men who made Casey famous! Here is the story, retold from folklore.

Casey Jones was an engineer on the Illinois Central Railroad's train, the Cannonball, that ran from Memphis, Tennessee, to Canton, Mississippi, and back. Casey was his nickname (his real name was John Luther Jones), his hometown was Cayce, Kentucky, and he could drive a train better than anyone else in the company. He could pull the whistle cord and make the old steam whistle moan out a tune as he came to crossings and trestles. He loved to wave at children as he passed their homes, and make his steam whistle sing as he went by a picnic full of local folks. Everybody loved Casey, and the men that worked with him admired him greatly.

On the night of April 29, 1900, Casey had brought the Cannonball into Memphis on time and was ready to hit the sack for some sleep when he heard that a friend was ill, and there was no one to drive Engine No. 382 back to Canton. Tired as he was, Casey volunteered to take the run, and his good friend "Simp" Webb offered to go along.

Simpson Webb and Casey pulled out of Memphis an hour and a half behind schedule and began to "highball." On the old-fashioned train signals along the track, a colored ball posted up high meant it was clear on the tracks ahead, so "highballing" meant running as fast as the engine could. Old No. 382 was pulling a freight train, so the high speed didn't put anyone in danger except Simp and Casey.

Simp was the fireman, and he kept the steam engine running hot by shoveling coal into the fire under the steam boiler. Casey and Simp were singing, rolling through the black night at very high speed. Up ahead there was trouble brewing. There was another train on the same track, and the men on that train knew old No. 382 was coming up behind them. What they didn't know was that Casey was at the throttle, driving the train at full speed. The train in front came to a sidetrack, where one train could pull off and let another train pass, like the passing lane of a modern highway. The sidetrack left the main tracks, ran alongside them for a few hundred yards, then came back and rejoined the main tracks.

When the train ahead of Casey pulled off onto the sidetrack, the engineer discovered that his train was so long it wouldn't all fit on the sidetrack; part of it stuck out on the main tracks, right in the way of Casey's train. Quickly, that engineer sent a crewman running back along the tracks with a red flag, to signal old No. 382 to slow down. The plan was to pull the front train onto the sidetrack so that the caboose cleared, but the engine stuck out in the way. Then old No. 382 could pass the caboose and stop just short of the front engine. When old No. 382's train was stopped, the front train would back up on the sidetrack so that the engine pulled off the main track, and old No. 382 could go ahead, while the caboose of the front train stuck out harmlessly on the main track behind.

That was the plan.

But Casey was tired and it was about four in the morning, near Vaughan, Mississippi, and he apparently did not see the flagman waving his red flag to tell Casey to slow down. Old No. 382 and the train of freight cars it was pulling thundered past the flagman and roared toward the sidetrack, where part of the train in front stuck out and blocked the tracks.

Casey saw the tracks blocked ahead and hit his whistle to warn the train in front of him. With his other hand he pulled hard on the level that worked the air brakes, trying to stop his thousand tons of train before it hit the train ahead of him. The metal drive wheels of the engine stopped turning, and the huge train skidded along the track with metal screaming and millions of sparks flying off the rails.

Casey saw that he could not stop his train in time to avoid a wreck. He knew if he jumped from the train to save his own life, and let go of the air brakes, the wreck would be much worse than it would if he stayed aboard and kept pulling on the brake. But his friend didn't have to die. Casey ordered his good friend Simp Webb to jump. Simp didn't want to, but he respected Casey, and jumped. He knew that he would live to tell the story.

Old Number 382 crashed into the other train with a horrible tearing of metal and the explosion of the steam boiler. It was a terrible wreck, but it would have been worse if Casey hadn't stayed on the air brakes. Casey died with one hand on the whistle cord and one hand on the air brake lever. Simp knelt in the grass beside the track to pray and weep for his friend.

"Casey Jones"—The Song

Casey Jones's death would have been the end of the story if it hadn't been for Casey's two good friends. This is the story of how they made him America's most famous train engineer. The words to the song are resung from folklore.

In Canton, Mississippi, Casey had another friend, a man named Wallace Saunders, who worked for the railroad wiping down the engines. With details of the wreck from Simp Webb, "Wash" Saunders began to sing a song that he wrote. The song was happy and sad at the same time and the melody was one of the catchiest ever written. Everyone who heard Wash sing the song loved it, just as the folks along the railroad had loved Casey. The song was an instant hit all across the South.

Two nationally famous vaudeville performers, T. Lawrence Seibert and Edward Newton, heard the song in New Orleans, and added it to their act. But they made it a comedy song, which it had not been before, and people began to think these two men had written the song.

"Casey Jones" went on to become what many people say was the most popular song in America for two decades. A lot of incorrect ideas got started—that the front train was stalled, that Simp jumped out of cowardice, that the trains hit head on and many lives were lost—but, worst of all, the real author of this wonderful song was forgotten.

Dozens of verses have been added, and many versions of the tune have been sung, but a few folksong experts have saved the story of Wash Saunders, and maybe at least three of the verses he originally wrote. The song probably started out like this:

> Casey Jones was the engineer,
> Told his fireman not to fear,
> All he wanted was the boiler hot,
> T' run int' Canton 'bout four o'clock.
>
> On Sunday morning it was drizzlin' rain,
> Looked down the road an' saw a train.
> Casey said, "Best make a jump.
> Two locomotives and they're bound to bump!"

Casey Jones, I know him well,
Told the fireman to ring the bell.
Fireman jumped and said, "Good-bye!
Casey Jones, you're bound to die!"

In the Park and in the Dark

There are two places where young people especially like to share stories with each other: in the park when they are playing games together, and in the dark where they love to tell scary stories. This group of tales ranges from a Colonial horror story to the kinds of stories young people tell about today's scariest problems.

Some of these stories are serious, others are funny. But they all are the kinds of tales we like to hear and tell to each other—in the park and in the dark.

Jack and the Fish

Colonial American life is preserved in the living history programs of Colonial Williamsburg, a historical park that you can visit. Ways of doing things as they were done two centuries ago are demonstrated there, such as fishing with a seine and weir, a kind of hand-held fishnet. Here is a story about a boy from that long ago time and place, as told by Rex Ellis.

In the town of Williamsburg, Virginia, there once lived a young man by the name of Jack. In those days black people were slaves and most slaves did not have last names. Black people usually got one day off a week and that day was Sunday. That was the day that Jack would go fishing. He loved to fish. Didn't matter if he caught anything or not, he just loved to fish. He'd get his seine and weir or he'd just use his pole, and he would go down to Queen's Creek, which was about an hour away from where he lived, and he'd sit on his favorite side of the bank and fish.

Well, Jack's mother had just recently become a Christian, and one thing Christians are strict about is working on Sundays. Sunday was a day of rest, and you were supposed to rest. No working, no fishing, no nothing. So Jack's mother said, "Jack, I don't want you to go down to that creek anymore on Sundays because that's a day of rest."

Jack said, "Mama, I love to fish. I fish every Sunday and I'm gonna fish this Sunday, too."

She said, "Jack, I'm mighty afraid something is gonna happen to you. If you go fishing on Sunday it means we are disrespectin' the Lord. Something bad might happen to you."

Jack said, "Can't be nothin worse than being a slave. I'm going fishin'!"

Well, Sunday came and, just as he said, he got himself ready to go fishing. He went out to the yard and got a piece of cornbread his mother had just baked in the Dutch oven. He put the bread in a sack over his shoulder, got his fishing gear, and started out. Pretty soon he got to Queen's Creek.

He went to his favorite spot and sat down, baited his hook, threw his line in the water, and sat waiting. He figured it would take some time before he got his first bite, so he reached for his piece of cornbread. As he was about to take a taste of it, he felt a tug on his line. Well, Jack started pulling back on that line and he noticed that the line was real hard to pull. He put down his cornbread and pulled with both hands, but it seemed no matter how hard he pulled, he could not pull that line back. He pulled with all of his strength and he could not move that line.

Then all of a sudden the line started pulling him. Jack tried his best to pull back on the line, but the line continued to pull him toward the edge of the water. Jack decided whatever it was, he did not want to see it! He dropped his pole and started running toward home.

Before he could go five steps a voice came out of the water and said, "Stoooooop!"

Jack wanted to keep running, but he had to stop.

The voice said, "Tuuuuuurrrn arooooouuuuund."

Jack slowly turned around, even though he was trying with all his might not to.

The voice commanded, "Raaaaaisssse your hands!"

Jack wanted to keep his hands still, but he could not control them. He had to raise his hands; it was like they had a life of their own.

The voice said, "Drop your hands!"

Jack tried to resist, but he had to drop his hands.

Then the voice said, "Waaaaalk."

Jack wanted to scream, but he couldn't. He wanted to cry, but he couldn't. He wanted to run home to his mother, but he was under the power of the voice. He found himself walking toward the water to the spot where the voice was coming from, but he kept his eyes closed tightly so that he would not see whatever it was.

Once he got to the edge of the water the voice said, "Stoooooop."

Jack stopped, and the voice said, "Ooooooopen your eyes."

Jack tried with all his might to keep his eyes closed, but he found himself being compelled to open them.

Aaaaaaaagh! What he saw almost made him faint! The creature's left leg was made of seaweed and sticks, and bugs were coming out of it. The other leg was made of mud and oozed with blood. Its chest was like a fish's scales and snakes were poking out of it. When it smiled, maggots and worms came out of its mouth. But the worst part was its eyes. They burned red like the devil's.

Then the creature said, "Look dooooowwwn."

Jack looked down and … and … and … *his* left leg turned into seaweed, *his* right leg turned into mud and started bleeding. Snakes poked out of *his* chest, bugs came out of *his* mouth, and *his* eyes burned red!

The voice said, "Look uuuuuuup."

Jack looked up and the creature had turned into Jack!

And the creature said, "Since you love to fish, you live with them—and I'll live with men."

Jack has not been heard of from that day to this. You know, nobody goes down to Queen's Creek much anymore to fish.

And *nobody* goes down there on Sundays.

Tillie

There are many versions of this scary tale, a favorite of young readers. This one is retold from the stories of Tyrone Wilkerson.

There was a girl named Tillie Williams who lived in a big, big house on Willy-Nilly Street. She had so many friends and relatives who gave her gifts every year on her birthday that the gifts began to sort of pile up. Her mother got angry and moved Tillie up into the attic, which was huge, because she and her gifts had outgrown her old room. Her Dad had threatened to get rid of some of her stuff, but now she wouldn't have to throw anything away.

Ever.

Now, the attic was pretty nice. She had her bed and her dresser and a desk for her to do her homework. The only thing Tillie didn't like about her big attic room was the fact that she had to climb those eight creaky, scary stairs every night to go to bed. She couldn't stand that. Every morning she'd get up and go downstairs and go to school. After that she'd come home and eat supper and watch TV and then ... she'd have to climb those stairs.

But, she had all her stuff upstairs—all her tapes and CDs and dolls and stuffed animals and posters and big pillows and stuff—you know, *stuff!* So, one night, she was complaining about having to go up those stairs, and her father went up with her to tell her a scary bedtime story.

After awhile, her father turned out the light and went slowly down the creaky stairs, and Tillie went to sleep. As she was falling asleep, she said out loud to herself, "I hate climbing those old stairs. I wish something would come and *get me out of this old attic!*"

And then she went to sleep.

In the middle of the night she woke up and heard, "Tillie ... "

She opened one eye and peeked out into the dark. "Dad," she whispered, "is that you?"

"Tillie!"

"Dad!" Tillie said. "Stop playing!"

"Tillie!" said the voice. "I'm on the *first* step and I'm coming to get you!"

Tillie put the blankets over her head.

"Tillie!!" said the voice in the dark. "I'm on the *second* step and I'm coming to get you!"

Tillie shook under the blankets. "If this is a joke, Dad, I'm going to be so mad at you!"

"Tillie!!! I'm on the *third* step and I'm coming to get you!"

"Oooo," said Tillie putting her fingers in her ears, "I hope he doesn't want my Janet Jackson tapes!"

"*Tillie!!!!* I'm on the *fourth* step and I'm coming to get you!"

Tillie went past the covers, past the comforter, all the way to the bottom of the bed.

"*Tillie!!!!!* I'm on the *fifth* step and I'm coming to get you!"

Tillie wasn't happy just being under the covers, and tried to get under the carpet.

"*Tillie!!!!!!* I'm on the *sixth* step and I'm coming to *get* you!"

She ran out from under the bed and piled her stuffed animals in her bed to make it look like she was sleeping there.

"*Tillie!!!!!!!* I'm on the *seventh* step and I'm coming to *get you!*"

Tillie got back out from under the bed and dragged her dresser over in front of the door.

"*Tillie!!!!!!!!* I'm on the *eighth* step and *I'm coming to get you!*"

Tillie heard the dresser fall over with a crash and heard the mirror break. "Serves you right!" she squealed in a whisper. "Seven years bad luck!"

"TILLIE!" said the voice right beside the bed …

"I GOT YOU!"

And then she woke up.

Johnny and the Liver

Stories that are both funny and scary—from ancient African tales of the returning dead to the centuries-old English story, "Golden Arm"—are favorites all over the world. Here is a modern-day story of this type, as told by Tyrone Wilkerson.

One day Johnny came home from school and his mother said to him, "Here's two dollars. Go to the corner store and get me some liver. Your father wants liver and onions for supper."

"Oh, no, Mom, not today. We're going to play football in that vacant lot down the street."

"Johnny," she said, "you go to that store and get that liver. Then you can go play football."

"Oh, Mom … "

"And don't you lose my money, either."

"Oh, all right, Mom." So Johnny went down the street, headed for the store. But he had to pass by the vacant lot where the guys were playing football.

They said, "Hey, Johnny! Come play quarterback for us." And, "Yeah, you're the best quarterback, Johnny." And, "Come on, Johnny, we're behind! Come on!"

"No," said Johnny, "I can't play. I've got to go to the store and get some liver for my family's dinner."

"You-all are having liver for dinner? Yucch!" said one friend.

"Come on, just throw a couple of passes and get our team ahead," said another.

"Oh ... all right," said Johnny. "Just a couple. Hut one, hut two ... " Johnny threw so many passes that soon his team was twenty points ahead. Then he said, "I've got to go! My mama's going to kill me!"

He ran to the store.

"Mr. Jones, I need two dollars worth of liver," he said in the store. Mr. Jones tore off a sheet of butcher paper and started to weigh out the liver.

Johnny reached into his pocket. "Oh, no! I lost the money while I was playing football." Mr. Jones stopped what he was doing and looked at Johnny sternly.

"Oh, Mr. Jones," Johnny said, "I've lost my mama's money. I don't know what I'm going to do. I've got two dollars at home. Mr. Jones, can you give me the liver and I'll run home with it and come right back with the two dollars?"

"No, no," said Mr. Jones, shaking his head. "I'm sorry, son, but I can't do business like that."

"But I've already been gone a long time, and my mama's going to wring my neck!"

"Now, son," said Mr. Jones, "you go home and get your two dollars, and then you come back and you can have the liver." He took the sheet of butcher paper off the scale and let it fall to the counter. Johnny picked up the empty paper and walked out of the store.

"Oh, what am I going to do?" said Johnny as he walked back past the vacant lot, still carrying the sheet of butcher paper.

All his friends came running over, saying "We won, Johnny, we won!" and, "What are you looking so sad for?"

"I lost my mama's money while I was playing football, and now I can't get the liver. I don't know what I'm going to do!"

"Oh," said his friends. "Tell you what. We can look for pop bottles and get the deposits." And, "We can look for some aluminum cans."

"No, no, that'll take too long!"

"Well ... " said one friend, "there is *one way* to get some liver."

"How?" asked Johnny.

"There's a fresh grave down at the cemetery!"

"Oh, barf!" said Johnny. "I'm not going to the cemetery to get liver for me and my mama and my daddy to eat! I ain't going to eat any!"

"It's either that," said his tough friend, "or face your mama!"

There was a long pause.

"Oh, all right."

Some of his friends started rapping, "Going to the cemetery! Going to the cemetery! Going to the cemetery!" And off they all went.

Inside the cemetery, they went looking for a freshly dug grave, with a mound of dirt that was still soft. They looked over here. They looked over there. Then they saw one.

They dug and dug and dug.

"There's the coffin. Open it up!"

"You open it," said Johnny.

"You're the one who needs the liver," said his friends, all hiding behind him.

They opened the lid: *crrreeeeaaaakkk …*

"Oh, yuchh! It's an ugly old man in there!"

"All right," said his friend, "cut him open. Use your pocketknife."

"Say, what?"

"Cut him open!"

"Oh, all right … YUCCH!" Johnny cut him open, took out the liver, and put it in the paper he had from the store. "Oh, man! This is gross!"

They slammed the lid down, piled the dirt back on, and ran out of the cemetery as fast as they could. As Johnny ran home, his mother stood waiting on the front porch, tapping her foot.

"Where is that boy? He's been gone an hour! It's just three blocks to the store."

When he ran up onto the porch, she said, "Where have you been? Give me that. Get in here! You go upstairs to your room. You'll have no dinner tonight!"

Johnny didn't want any dinner tonight, anyway. He knew what that was! He went up to his room and went to bed at ten o'clock. At midnight he could sneak down and make himself a sandwich.

His father came home, his mother cooked the liver, and they ate it. They thought it smelled bad, even for liver and onions, but that's all.

Ten o'clock came ... eleven o'clock came ... everyone was in bed. Johnny was sneaking out of bed to go get a sandwich when suddenly he heard something out in his front yard.

Just as the church bell was ringing midnight, a voice said, "Johhhnnnyyy, Johhhnnnyyy ... "

Johnny ran to the door of his room and looked out. He even looked in the closet.

"Johhhnnnyyy!"

He opened the window and looked all over the front yard. There was the old, ugly dead man, standing in his front yard, holding his side. He was pointing his old, bony fingers up toward Johnny and saying, "Johhhnnnyyy. I waaant my liiivvveeerrr."

"I don't have your old liver," Johnny whispered as loud as he could.

"Johhhnnnyyy!"

"My mama and my daddy ate your liver for dinner. Now get out of my yard."

"Johhhnnnyyy!"

"Shut up! You're going to wake up my mama and my daddy."

"Johhhnnnyyy. I waaant my liiivvveeerrr."

"*I told you,*" Johnny yelled, then he whispered, "I told you, I don't have your old liver!"

"Johhhnnnyyy ... at miiidnight tomooorrow ... I'll be baaack ... to get my liiivvveeerrr ... " Then he went back to the cemetery.

Johnny didn't sleep at all that night. He tossed and turned. He got tangled up in the covers and thought somebody was trying to strangle him. When the sun came up he was exhausted.

He met his friends at the school bus stop and grabbed his tough friend. "Do you know what happened to me last night?"

"Yeah," his friend guessed, "you got a whipping!"

"No!" yelled Johnny, shaking his friend by his coat collar. "Worse than that!"

"What could be worse than a whipping?"

"That old dead man came to my house last night!"

"No, he didn't!"

"Yes, he did, too," said Johnny. "He wanted his old liver. And he's coming back tonight, too!"

"Oh, boy, can we come and watch?"

"No!" Johnny yelled. "This is serious!"

Johnny couldn't do anything right in school that day. He couldn't remember where Antarctica was. He couldn't divide sixty by five. He was lost.

But at the end of the day he knew what he had to do. After school he gathered all his friends that had been with him the day before.

"All right, you guys," he said, "you have to help me. You got me into this."

"All right, what do we have to do?"

"We've got to go back," said Johnny, "and get some more liver for that old dead man."

His friends said, "To the cemetery? That was fun!" And they rapped, "Going to the cemetery! Going to the cemetery! Going to the cemetery!"

Back at the cemetery, they looked around for another freshly dug grave, one with a mound of dirt on it, still soft. They looked over here. They looked over there. And then they found one.

They dug and they dug and they dug.

"There's the coffin."

"Open it up!"

"I opened the last one," said Johnny.

"And you're going to open up this one, too."

Crrreeeaaakkk...

"Oh! Yucch! Gross! Barf! It's an ugly old lady. She looks like a giant, old, dead prune!" said Johnny.

"Cut her open."

"I can't cut a lady open."

"Cut her open!"

"Oh, all right. Yucch! Let's see, that's a kidney. Double yucch! No butcher paper. Here, hold this."

They shut the lid and piled the dirt up and ran as fast as they could out of the cemetery.

Johnny's mama was on the front porch, saying, "Where is that boy? He's late getting home from school. Did he miss that bus?"

Johnny ran up onto the porch, kissed his mama and kind of missed her cheek and hit her ear, and ran upstairs. He waited all evening long, right beside the window. He said good night down the stairs to his mama and his daddy at ten o'clock, but he didn't go to bed. He just waited and waited. Ten o'clock came ... eleven o'clock ... everyone was in bed.

Then just as the church bell was ringing midnight, he heard, "Johhhnnnyyy."

Johnny opened the window. "What?"

"Johhhnnnyyy. I waaant my liiivvveeerrr."

Johnny took that lump of liver and threw it out the window.

"There's your liver, you old man, and now you get out of my yard!"

"Thaaannnkkk yooouuu." And the old man went back to the cemetery.

Johnny breathed a huge sigh of relief, and climbed in bed.

"Johhhnnnyyy." It was a higher voice. "Johhhnnnyyy."

Johnny jumped out of bed and ran to the open window and looked out.

It was the old woman, holding her side and pointing at him. "Johhhnnnyyy. I waaant *myyyyy* liiivvveeerrr." Her white dress was blowing in the wind.

"I don't have your old liver. Some old dead man's got it, and there he goes down the street!"

That old dead lady was *tough!* She ran down the street and caught up with that old man, and they were fighting and fighting over it. Johnny said, "I'll never eat liver again!" and went to bed.

But some people say those old dead folks stayed out of their graves too long, fighting over that liver, and the sunlight caught them. Now they can't get back in their graves.

And they're still wandering around, looking for their liver. So you'd better be careful. Some night you may go to bed ... and right at midnight ...

Somebody outside your window will say ...

Liiivvveeerrr ....

My Friend Bennie

*The most dangerous monster facing young people today
is the villain in this bettersweet story from Washington,
D.C., told by Rex Ellis.*

I just got back from the hospital
and I saw a terrible sight;
   my friend Bennie was there and
   I stayed with him most of the night.
   I had to leave a few minutes ago
   cause he'd taken a turn for the worse,
   and I got this weird feeling, that the next time I see
      him,
   he'll be riding in the back of a hearse.

Bennie and me have been best friends
since before I was five.
We lived on the same street corner,
'cept we lived on opposite sides.

Bennie and me shared everything

when we were growing up.
He watched my back ... I watched his,
we brought each other luck.

Like that time when Russell Jimmerson said,
"I'm gon' beat your tail!"
Bennie said, "Don't worry, I got a plan
and I know that it won't fail."
When Russell came at me that day after school,
the boys thought that I would run;
they didn't know that Bennie and me
was gon' have ourselves some fun.

Russell made his move, guess he thought he was
        cool,
by talkin about my mama.
I told him that at least the ma I had
didn't wear big ragged pajamas.
This got him mad and he took a swing
that almost reached my head.
But I ducked just in time and pushed him back
and he landed in a flower bed.

Old Bennie saw him fall from the third floor
        window
where he promised me he'd be.
He dropped a bag of manure on Russell's big head
and boy was he a sight to see!

That bag dropped down on him
and that manure came out,
and crowned ol' Russell king;

he jumped all around trying to shake it all down
and he looked like a puppet on a string.

The boys laughed so hard they fell on the ground,
and tears came from their eyes.
Ol' Russell would stand, and then fall again
cause that manure made him slip and slide.

Well, he ran to the bathroom as fast as he could
and ran water in the sink;
but that didn't help cause the smell was spreading
and Russell was starting to stink.

So he ran on home and stayed there alone
until his daddy arrived;
and they tell me when his father asked him what
    had happened
Russell looked down and he lied.

After that day everyone knew
if you messed with either of us,
one would find a way to help the other
and we'd get you back or bust.

Benny and me was like red beans and rice;
we naturally went together
and I guess I was foolish but I chose
to believe we'd stay that way forever.

So you can imagine my surprise when they called
    me last month
and told me my buddy was sick;

and when they told me it was drugs that he had
     been takin,
I thought someone was playin' a trick.

See, Bennie and me shared everything,
the good news and the bad,
but he never told me about those drugs
and that's what made me so sad.

Maybe if I'd known it, I could have helped him
     out.
At least I could have talked to him;
together we could have figured what it was all
     about
but Bennie never let me in.

I've been thinking about this thing for days and
     days,
it's been so hard for me to take—
Why didn't he tell me, why didn't he try?
Didn't he know that his life was at stake?

Its hard to watch someone you love tremblin' and
     moanin' in pain,
but it's worse if you think that you could've
     stopped
that life from going down the drain.
I don't know if Bennie will ever be well;
They say drugs will make you a slave.
But if it happens to you, think it through and
     through,
don't neglect a life *you* might save.

Brother Rabbit and His Friends Today

The African animal fables and trickster stories have added tremendously to American literature and are loved by Americans of all origins. These stories have been told in the United States, especially in the homes of Southerners, for four centuries. The tales have been updated by each generation that told them, and today's versions are just as much fun as those told long ago in Africa.

This pair of fables shows how Brother Rabbit and his friends continue today to be a source of wisdom and laughter for young readers of all ethnic groups in America.

The Cabbage Inspector

This modern yarn, as told by Tyrone Wilkerson, is a version of "Brother Rabbit and Brother Farmer," also known as "Brother Rabbit in the Cabbage Patch." It also is a retelling of the central event in "Brother Rabbit's Cool Air Swing."

One day Brother Rabbit was hungry. From the top of a hill at the edge of the woods he could see the garden of a farmer nearby. The garden was enclosed by a high, rabbit-proof fence. Right in the middle of the garden was the cabbage patch. Right in the middle of the cabbage patch was the biggest cabbage in the world. The farmer was trying to get in the *Book of World Records* for being the biggest cabbage.

"Mmmm-mmmm," said Brother Rabbit. "What I wouldn't give for just one bite of that giant cabbage."

He hopped home and put on his Sunday-go-to-meeting clothes. He put on a tie, got his briefcase, and went to the farm at the edge of the woods.

The farmer's daughter had one job for the summer. It was her job to guard that world's-record-size cabbage. She had to sit at the gate of the garden and make sure no one came in and stole that cabbage. It was a boring job, but someone had to do it.

Brother Rabbit came hopping down the lane with his briefcase. "Look out, look out," he said. "I'm the cabbage inspector. Open up the gate and let me in to inspect that cabbage."

Well, the girl saw that the rabbit had on a suit and tie and was carrying a briefcase, so she thought he must be someone important. She let him in the garden.

As he hopped out of sight he said, "When the sun is straight up high—at twelve o'clock—open up and let me out. I've got other gardens to inspect!"

When he was in the middle of the patch he couldn't be seen from the gate. He set his briefcase down. He climbed up on the cabbage and took hold of the top of one huge leaf. He slid down the cabbage, peeling the leaf off as he slid. It was just like a playground slide with a buffet at the bottom!

"Wheeeee!" said Brother Rabbit as he slid down. Then he ate that leaf. He climbed back up to the top and took hold of another leaf.

"Wheeeee!" said Brother Rabbit as he slid down, peeling that leaf off. Then he ate it up.

About thirty "wheeeees!" and thirty leaves later, Brother Rabbit was so full he couldn't climb back up. He just nibbled on the leaves at the bottom. At high noon, he tried to hop back to the gate, but all he could do was waddle.

"Look out! (Burp!) Look out! (Belch!)" said Brother Rabbit as he waddled out the gate. "Twelve o'clock. More gardens to inspect." The daughter let him out and he waddled away.

After doing this for four days, that little skinny rabbit was a little fat rabbit! And that giant round cabbage was just a little white, normal-size cabbage. The farmer came out to hoe the cabbage patch, and he saw that his world's-record-size cabbage had gone on a diet!

"Has somebody been in here eating on my cabbage?" he said to his daughter.

"Oh, Daddy," she said, "nobody's been here but the cabbage inspector."

"What did he look like?"

"Well, he's kind of short," she said, "and he has real tall pink-and-white ears. He must have been inspecting the cotton fields, too. He had a little piece of cotton stuck on the back of his coat. I was going to take it off for him, but I was scared it might embarrass him."

"Daughter! Don't you know what a rabbit looks like?"

"Was *that* a rabbit?" she asked. "Do rabbits get fatter after twelve o'clock?"

"I'm going to send you to school for *twenty-four hours*, so you can learn what a rabbit looks like."

"Oh, please, Daddy, don't do that!"

"Well," said the father, "the next time he comes here, you let him in. Then you come and tell me."

"Are you going to get him, Daddy?"

"Yeah, we're going to have rabbit and cabbage stew!"

The girl began to sing:

"Daddy's going to get that rabbit!
Daddy's going to get that rabbit!
Daddy's going to get that rabbit!"

Sure enough, the next day, along came the cabbage inspector again.

"Look out, look out! I'm the cabbage inspector; let me in!"

"Okaaaaaayyyyy," said the girl, opening the gate, and as Brother Rabbit hopped in she was humming:

"Hm-hmmmm hmmmm-hm hmm hmmm hmm-hmm!

Daddy's going to hmm hmmm hmm-hmm!
Hm-hmmmm hmmmm-hm hmm hmmm rabbit!

Down in the cabbage patch, Brother Rabbit said, "Whee!"

The girl ran and got her father. "He's down there, Daddy. Go get him!" The farmer got his shotgun and down the lane they went.

"Daddy's going to get that rabbit!
Daddy's going to get that rabbit!
Daddy's going to get that rabbit!"

Down at the patch, "Whee!"

Pretty soon the farmer was standing right behind Brother Rabbit. He tapped the rabbit on the shoulder with the barrel of his shotgun. Brother Rabbit turned and looked up the barrel of that gun and he started to do his best act.

"Oh, p-p-p-lease, Brother Man," he said, "don't shoot me. I've got a wife and ... " He thought about it. " ... twenty-seven kids!"

Well, the farmer took Brother Rabbit and tied up his paws. Then he tied him upside-down to a tree branch that hung over the lane, as a warning to other rabbits. The hot summer sun burned down on Brother Rabbit and he started to sweat. The wind began to blow and Brother Rabbit started to swing.

Brother Rabbit said, "Oh, woe is me! I'm a goner. I'll die up here. Heaven, here I come."

Then he started to sing:

"I'm going to heaven in a swing, swing, swing!
I'm going to heaven in a swing, swing, swing!
I'm going to heaven in a swing, swing, swing!"

Just about then, Brother Bear came along the path. He saw Brother Rabbit hanging up in that tree.

"Brother Rabbit," said Brother Bear, "what are you doing hanging up in that tree?"

"I'm going to heaven in a swing, swing, swing!
I'm going to heaven in a swing, swing, swing!
I'm going to heaven in a swing, swing, swing!"

"Well," said Brother Bear, "I know you didn't tie yourself up in that tree like that. Who put you up there?"

"Well," said Brother Rabbit, "Brother Man put me up here for stealing his cabbage. But, you know what? I'm getting mighty thirsty. Would you take my place up here for just a minute? Long enough for me to go down to the river and get a drink?"

"Well," said Brother Bear, "I don't know about that!"

"But this is so good for your circulation," said Brother Rabbit. "It gets the blood down to your brain. And besides, we've been together through thick and thin. I'd do the same for you. Come on. Just for a little while!"

"Oh, okay," said Brother Bear.

Brother Bear took Brother Rabbit down and untied his paws. Then Bear climbed up the tree and sat on a branch. He tied himself up and swung down over the path. He was so heavy that the branch bent way down, and Brother Bear's head bumped the ground every once in a while.

Brother Rabbit waved goodbye and ran down to the river. After he got a drink, he went home and took a nap. After a while the hot sun beat down on Bear, and the wind started blowing him from side to side. He hit his head against the tree every once in a while.

Then he started to sing:

"Let's see … what was Brother Rabbit singing? Oh, yeah … " His head hit the tree and he began to hear bells.

"I'm going to heaven singing ding-dong-ding!
I'm going to heaven singing ding-dong-ding!
I'm going to heaven singing ding-dong-ding!"

He was so excited he couldn't even remember the words to the song.

Pretty soon the farmer heard the bear singing. He came up the lane and looked at Brother Bear.

He said, "Brother Bear, what are you doing up there in that tree?"

Brother Bear said:

"I'm going to heaven singing ding-dong-ding!

I'm going to heaven singing ding-dong-ding!
I'm going to heaven singing ding-dong-ding!"

The farmer yelled, "Don't you know it's not right to take somebody else's punishment? I'll fix you!" He pulled out his big, sharp pocket knife. The bear could just see that knife shining in the sun.

"Oh, Brother Man," said Brother Bear, "don't cut me when I'm hanging upside down in this tree!"

The farmer reached up there and cut Brother Bear down. He landed on the ground with a thud. Then he cut the rope off the bear's front paws, and off his back paws. That bear rolled upright and started running on all fours. The farmer broke a branch off the tree and chased the bear clear to the woods, switching him with the branch all the way.

Brother Bear was so mad he vowed that if he caught that rabbit he'd pull his ears off. He'd pull that cotton tail off. He'd turn that rabbit's head around so it faced east when he was going west! But Brother Rabbit got away—he moved to the next county!

Brother Possum and Brother Snake

This tale is retold from a story which Mary Furlough tells. It is difficult to create on the printed page the excitement and characterizations that the human voice gives to a story told out loud. The nervousness of Brother Possum and the hissing cunning of Brother Snake are recreated here in writing to bring the reader some of the wonderful variety in the teller's voice.

Brother Possum was walking near the highway one day. He passed a lot of other possums who had not managed to get across the road in traffic. They were now very flat possums. He was so interested in all those flat possums that he walked right onto Brother Snake and didn't see him.

"Sssss," said Brother Snake, "ssssso would you help me?"

Brother Possum jumped about ten feet in the air, turned around twice, and ran and hid behind a tree. He looked at Brother Snake. Brother Snake was lying beside the road with a brick on top of him. It was the strangest thing he had ever seen.

"H–h–h–how did you get that brick on top of you?" asked Brother Possum meekly.

"Sssssomeone drove a brick truck by and a brick bounced off and landed on me," said Brother Snake. "Sssso would you help me?"

"N–n–n–no," said Brother Possum, "you'd bite me."

"Sssssurely you don't think I'd bite you after you'd helped me!"

"W–w–w–well," said Brother Possum, "I'll bet you would!"

"Sssscertainly not. Just ssssssneak out here and lift this brick off me."

"O–o–o–oh, okay," said Brother Possum, and he ran out to the snake, took the brick off, and ran back behind the tree and hid.

The snake didn't move a muscle. "Sssssee?" he said. "I wouldn't hurt you after you'd helped me."

Brother Possum came out from behind the tree a little bit.

"Sssso come on back," said the snake. "Let's be friends."

Brother Possum came a little closer.

The snake seemed to be looking at the brick very closely, not even looking at the possum. Brother Possum came a little closer.

The snake turned and bit him! Brother Possum let out a yelp, but the snake held on with his sharp fangs. Just then Brother Rabbit came along.

"Howdy, Brother Possum. Howdy, Brother Snake. Nice day," said Brother Rabbit.

"H-h-h-howdy," said Brother Possum nervously.

"Hmmmmm hmmmmm," said Brother Snake, with a mouthful of possum.

Brother Rabbit tilted his head to one side and looked at the snake. "What for are you biting on Brother Possum?"

"Hmmm hmmmmhm hm hmmmm hmm," said Brother Snake.

"I can't understand you," said Brother Rabbit. "Speak up!"

"HMMM HMMMMHM HM HMMMM HMM," said Brother Snake.

"What was that?" said brother Rabbit. "What'd you say?"

"I'M GOING TO EAT HIM!" said Brother Snake, opening his mouth. Brother Possum shot around behind Brother Rabbit faster than the blink of an eye.

"Well, why didn't you say so," said Brother Rabbit, acting unconcerned. "How'd you catch him, anyway?"

"He was taking a brick off my back," said Brother Snake.

"Say, what?" asked Brother Rabbit.

"He was taking a brick off my back."

Brother Rabbit just laughed and laughed. "You must think I'm pretty stupid if you think I'll believe that!"

"It's true," said Brother Snake.

"No, it's not," said Brother Rabbit. "That could never happen. How could a brick get on your back?"

"It fell off a brick truck."

"No, it didn't!"

"Yes, it did!"

"Now, you'd have to *show* me that brick … "

"It's right here, you stupid rabbit!"

"*That* brick?" asked Brother Rabbit.

"Yes! It landed on my back," said Brother Snake.

"Where?"

"Right here."

"*No* … "

"Yes, it did, you stupid rabbit!"

"Now, you'd have to *show* me that!"

"I was right here … " said Brother Snake, crawling back to where he'd been, beside the brick.

"And that brick was on your back … " said Brother Rabbit, picking the brick up and looking it over, "What? Like this?" He set the brick on top of the snake.

"Yes! You stupid rabbit! Just like that! Now do you believe me?"

"Why, yes, Brother Snake," said Brother Rabbit. "I *do!* Brother Possum, let's go eat some greens."

Then Brother Rabbit and Brother Possum walked off down the road and left Brother Snake under that brick, hissing mad.

I was by that way just the other day, and he's still there!

About the Storytellers

- *Aunt Hattie* was the Indian-Negro cook and nurse in the family of Betty Shamburger Atwood, who passed Aunt Hattie's story to her own grandniece, Texas folklorist Peggy Shamburger Hendricks. Peggy in turn passed the story to her cousins, the editors of this collection. Aunt Hattie was a wonderful lady and fine storyteller, and many families have passed her stories down from generation to generation. "Wham! Slam! Jenny-Mo-Jam!" is the only Aunt Hattie story of which these editors are currently aware. The story is sometimes told about a boy named Barney McCabe, or about Wylie (who met the Hairy Man in another story) and his sister.

- *Len Cabral* is a nationally acclaimed storyteller living in Cranston, Rhode Island. He has been working professionally since the early 1980s throughout the United States and Canada, appearing at the Smithsonian Institution and as a featured teller at the National Storytelling Festival and other festivals nationwide. His strong Cape Verdean ancestry comes alive in the telling of Cape Verdean, African, and Caribbean folktales. He tells tales from around the world using mime, poetry, song, humor, and vivid characterizations to all ages at schools, libraries, museums, hospitals, and festivals. Len received the Jefferson Award, co-founded both the Sidewalk Storytellers and The Spellbinders, and is a director on the Rhode Island State Arts Council and a regional advisor to the board of the National Association for the Preservation and Perpetuation of Storytelling (NAPPS).

- *Rex Ellis,* Ed.D., is the Director of the Office of Museums Programs at the Smithsonian Institution, and was formerly the director of the Department of African-American Interpretation and Presentations at the Colonial Williamsburg Foundation. Educated at Virginia Commonwealth University, Wayne State University, and the College of William and Mary, Rex has performed historical tours, theatrical vignettes, children's programs, and storytelling at museums, foundations, and festivals. He is a member of the Screen Actors' Guild, AFTRA, the Association of Black Storytellers, and other national organizations, and has served as the president of the board of directors of NAPPS.

- *Mary Furlough* has been telling stories professionally since 1984 and is called upon frequently to share her stories at libraries, schools, university storytelling conferences, and summer camps for the gifted and talented. As Head of Children's Services at William F. Laman Public Library in North Little Rock, Arkansas, she is able to incorporate storytelling into her multifaceted job. She is an active member of the Arkansas Library Association. Her specialties are mountain stories and Br'er Rabbit stories.

   Mary grew up near Arkadelphia, Arkansas, and graduated from Henderson State University. She and her husband live in Little Rock and have three grown children.

- *Sarah McCoy* was born on a farm called the King and Anderson Plantation outside of Clarksdale, Mississippi, and grew up hearing stories from her parents and grandparents. She lived in Grand Rapids, Michigan, for fifteen years, working in children's services for the Grand Rapids Public Library for ten of those years. She left the library in 1985 to tell stories full-time.

   Sarah now lives in Trotwood, Ohio, where she continues to tell stories full-time. Sarah serves on the roster of Artists for Young Audiences of Greater Cleveland, Inc., and appears at storytelling festivals around the nation.

- *Miss Lou* is *Louise Bennett,* born in Kingston, Jamaica, and educated at St. Simon's College and Excelsior College, and at the Royal Academy of Dramatic Art in England. Miss Lou has been awarded the M.B.E., the Order of Jamaica, and received the Gold Musgrave Medal in 1978. She is the leading folklore performing artist in Jamaican storytelling. While none of her stories are included in this collection, her dialect versions of famous Anansi stories have served as the inspiration for the interpretation of stories from Jamaica found in this anthology.

- *Jackie Torrence* was born in Granite Quarry, North Carolina, and now lives in Salisbury, North Carolina. She leaves her home about 270 days a year to tell her stories of Jack and his adventures, stories about Br'er Rabbit, mountain tales, stories about mysteries, ghosts and legends, and great blues musicians. Jackie has told in every kind of venue from Lincoln Center in New York City to the East-West Center in Honolulu. She has told at hundreds of colleges, universities, fairs, festivals, conferences, and conventions. Her recordings have won honors from the Parent's Choice Award to the American Library Association Notable Record Award. She has been described in the national press as the most highly honored storyteller in America today.

- *Tyrone Wilkerson,* a poet, playwright, actor, director, and storyteller, travels the nation and his home state of Oklahoma as an artist in the schools for the State Board of Education, as an artist-in-residence for the State Arts Council of Oklahoma, and for the Tulsa Arts and Humanities Council/Harwelden Institute. He was one of the founding members of the Territorial Storytellers, the first such organization in Oklahoma.

  Tyrone feels his specialty of Southern folklore and African-American "Br'er Rabbit Tales" helps keep the oral tradition of lesson-teaching alive in spite of television. He states, "Good storytellers nowadays are historians preserving the cultures of many ethnic groups."

- *Lloyd Wilson* was born in Wilmington, North Carolina. He was introduced to storytelling and music at a very young age, thanks to the lullabies and bedtime stories that were sung and told to him by his mother. His dedication to music and his fascination with the power of the spoken word prompted him to begin his research into African and African-American storytelling's own roots.

  He learned of the *griot,* the African village storyteller and keeper of the folk wisdom of his people. He developed a characterization of the *griot* to show American young people how African children were taught the ways of their people. His performances include percussion demonstrations, audience participation, and the telling of folktales with musical accompaniment for effect and color.

  Lloyd's storytelling spectrum ranges from the most traditional of stories to the most modern, from all parts of the world. He appears at festivals and storytelling conferences throughout the nation.